DO

Abner Buell was world video game champion. He could annihilate anyone at any electronic contest ever devised—including all the ones he had invented to reap billions in profit while reveling in bright bursts of perverse pleasure. Now there was only one game left for Abner to create and then conquer all opposition: a game that turned men into killer pawns, women into wantons, and the great powers of the world into dead-certain nuclear suicides.

Remo Williams, the Destroyer, and his Oriental mentor Chiun, had to pull Buell's plug before Buell punched the ultimate key to catastrophe. But how could they win out over this fiendish wizard when Buell crossed enough circuits to program Chiun to destroy the Destroyer . . . ?

——THE DESTROYER #60——
THE END OF THE GAME

SIGNET Mysteries You'll Enjoy

The Destroyer #60
THE END OF THE GAME

WARREN MURPHY & RICHARD SAPIR

A SIGNET BOOK

NEW AMERICAN LIBRARY

PUBLISHER'S NOTE

This novel is a work of fiction. Names, characters, places, and incidents either are the product of the author's imagination or are used fictitiously, and any resemblance to actual persons, living or dead, events, or locales is entirely coincidental.

NAL BOOKS ARE AVAILABLE AT QUANTITY DISCOUNTS WHEN USED TO PROMOTE PRODUCTS OR SERVICES. FOR INFORMATION PLEASE WRITE TO PREMIUM MARKETING DIVISION, NEW AMERICAN LIBRARY, 1633 BROADWAY, NEW YORK, NEW YORK 10019.

SIGNET TRADEMARK REG. U.S. PAT. OFF. AND FOREIGN COUNTRIES REGISTERED TRADEMARK—MARCA REGISTRADA HECHO EN CHICAGO, U.S.A.

SIGNET, SIGNET CLASSIC, MENTOR, PLUME, MERIDIAN AND NAL BOOKS are published by New American Library, 1633 Broadway, New York, New York 10019

First Printing, February, 1985

1 2 3 4 5 6 7 8 9

PRINTED IN THE UNITED STATES OF AMERICA

Chapter One

Waldo Hammersmith believed that none of the good things in life was free. Everything in the world cost. You paid for what you got and sometimes you paid double and sometimes you didn't get anything to begin with and still paid double.

That was what he always said. But if Waldo Hammersmith had really believed his good advice instead of using it just to cry about his misfortunes, he might one day not be looking very closely at a .38 Police Special. It would be held by a detective.

The detective would be telling him to do something illegal. Waldo Hammersmith would not believe him.

"Aw, c'mon. This has got to be a game," Waldo would say.

He would see a bright flash coming out of the barrel. He would have no time to disbelieve that he was being shot because that portion of the human anatomy that was in charge of disbelieving was covering the wall behind his blown-open head.

It was too late for Waldo. Everything was too late for Waldo because he had been played to perfection,

as if someone somewhere had a schematic diagram of
his soul and had pressed all the right buttons to make
him do what he was supposed to do.

It had all started one wintry morning, when Waldo
Hammersmith had begun to believe that he was getting something for nothing.

It came in the mail. Ordinarily, Waldo opened the
bills last. But this day, he opened those envelopes
first. The credit card for gas had hit almost a hundred
dollars that month. He had driven his wife, Millicent,
to her mother's twice. Her mother lived far out on
Long Island and the Hammersmiths lived in the Bronx.
Waldo grumbled over the bill, then decided there
might be a small benefit in it. When he showed it to
his wife, they might decide not to visit her mother
that often.

There were other bills. There was heating that was
too high. A general charge bill that he had thought he
had held down but which had come booming back
with an old charge he had forgotten. There was the
rent and the partial payment on the medical insur-
ance and the totals came to roughly twenty-five dollars more that month than he brought home in legal
salary.

Waldo Hammersmith lived in terror of the Internal
Revenue Service computers somehow putting those
two things together. He drove a cab and while he
reported most of his normal tips, he did not report
what kept his nostrils barely above sea level—those
five- and ten-dollar bills he got when he would drive a
passenger to any sexual delight he might want.

That was the real reason he worked the International Terminal at Kennedy. He would get both a tip
from the passenger and a small cut from the brothel,

and thus he did, by daily crime, barely make it. If Millicent didn't lose her job.

Waldo went through his bills like someone suspecting a cancer in his personal economy, something that eventually must be fatal but had so far been kept miraculously under control by the sudden strange lusts of Pakistanis or Nigerians waving hundred-dollar bills and looking for a good time.

He saved his Insta-Charge bill for last. It allowed him what he called his no-bounce security. He could write a check for more than he had in his account and the bank treated the overdraft as a loan.

When he took it out, he was assured by the bank that it was a security blanket. But the security blanket lasted only two months before Waldo Hammersmith was at his credit limit, and he went back to bouncing checks again every so often.

In the long run, it had just been a loan, just another one that Waldo Hammersmith, forty-two, kept servicing. It seemed that out of his little cab he was servicing the entire financial world. And not quite making it.

Then he opened the Insta-Charge statement to see how much that security blanket which was no longer there was costing him to service. The number was right. More than fourteen hundred dollars. But they had the symbol wrong. They had a plus where a minus should be.

"They'll catch it," he told himself. Mistakes this good just did not happen to Waldo Hammersmith. He wondered if he should report it or let them catch it themselves.

He would ignore it. He would pretend it just did not happen, because you always paid for what you got.

But the next day he was driving his cab past the

bank branch and he thought that perhaps the bank had made an error that no one would ever catch. It happened sometimes, so he parked and went into the bank.

Nervously, he presented his Insta-Charge card to the teller and asked her for his balance. And he was told that he had $1,485 in his account. Adding in his security margin, he could write a check for almost three thousand dollars.

He was sweating when he left the bank. He immediately drove to another branch of the same bank and a different teller gave him the same good news. He had almost three thousand dollars of available cash.

The bank had made a mistake. Maybe they would catch it, but it certainly wasn't his fault and he wasn't going to go to jail over it. So he paid his bills. He took Millicent out to dinner. With the three thousand dollars of available cash, he got through the month whistling.

Then came the new bank statement. Waldo Hammersmith couldn't believe the computer numbers. He had almost three thousand dollars cash in his account and a total of forty-five hundred available, counting the security blanket.

He wrote a check for four thousand dollars. He stood at the teller's window as she checked his identity, went up to the branch manager, and then returned. She had that cold face behind the window, the kind of face that had said "no" to him all his life.

"How do you want it, sir?" she asked.

"Any way you want to give it."

"Tens, twenties, fifties, hundreds?" she asked.

"Hundreds," said Waldo. The words almost choked him. He tried to look calm. He tried to look like a man who ordinarily took four thousand dollars from his bank account.

He bought himself three new suits, cleaned up every last bill, got a new television and tape deck and one of those video games that kids were supposed to enjoy.

"Waldo, where are you getting the money from?" asked Millicent. She was a dumpy fireplug of a woman who wore print dresses and hats with fruit on them. Millicent had what Waldo felt was an insatiable sexual appetite. Once a month, without fail.

Waldo performed for Millicent because she would become unbearable when denied access to manly services. He had hoped she would consider cheating on him but decided that the only man who might want her was a drunk seventeen-year-old laced with aphrodisiacs. Blind wouldn't help all that much because even hands could feel the multitude of cellulite lumps on Millicent's body.

On the street Waldo could tell where Millicent's head was because it had the ugly hat on it. In the bedroom, he never found it that easy.

"I asked you where you got the money, Waldo."

"None of your business."

"Is it illegal, Waldo? Tell me that. Are you doing something illegal?"

"You're damned right," he said.

Millicent turned back to the new color television set. "Keep it up. It's wonderful," she said.

The next month Waldo Hammersmith bought himself a new car with a check. The month after that he purchased his own taxicab with the medallion license worth five times the price of the cab itself. The month after that, he purchased two more cabs and hired other drivers for them.

The following month he sold the two cabs because the only way he wanted to deal with taxi drivers was from the back seat, giving them directions. That is, when his chauffeur was ill. Waldo had so much money from his growing Insta-Charge account, he moved from the Bronx to Park Avenue.

Millicent settled for a lump-sum divorce. She took the kids, and Waldo lived alone with closets full of clothes and new video games and television sets which he bought like he used to buy cigarettes. There had obviously been a computer error which was not going to be changed because only the computer knew. He didn't care whether the money was being taken out of someone else's account or out of some computer calculation somewhere or whatever. It was just there, some sort of grand welfare.

By year's end, it was no longer a gift or an error but his natural right. He found it very normal that every time he spent all the money in his account, it came back doubled and tripled.

And then it stopped growing. He almost phoned the bank to complain. The following month, it shrank. And then he got the first phone call.

It was a woman's voice, soft and massaging.

"We're so sorry that your funds have shrunk. Would you come in and pay us a visit?"

"My funds haven't shrunk. Everything is fine," he said. "What's wrong?"

"Nothing. We just want to talk to you. Maybe you can use more money?"

"No, I'm fine," Waldo said. "Who is this?" His heart fell. They had found out. It was inevitable and now it had happened. Now they knew and Waldo Hammersmith was done for.

"Waldo," said the voice as beautiful as silver chimes.

"Please don't play games. If there is one thing I hate, it is a person who plays games. Waldo, come in and we will get you some more money."

"Who are you?"

"Waldo, you have taken $1.47 million that is not yours."

"That much?" said Waldo. He could have sworn it was only a few hundred thousand but he had stopped counting. Why continue to count when you had all the money you wanted?

"That much, Waldo." The woman's voice was creamy smooth. Almost too smooth, Waldo thought. Almost mechanical.

"I didn't know it was that much," Waldo said. "I swear I didn't know it was that much."

The time had come to answer for the funds. The address the woman had given him was a bare office. The door was unlocked. Inside was one chair which faced a blank wall. It felt like a prison already.

"Hello, Waldo," came that beautiful voice. But she wasn't in the room.

"Stop looking for a loudspeaker, Waldo, and listen to me. You have had a good life recently, haven't you?"

"Not bad," Waldo said. It had been glorious. He felt his hands grow wet with sweat and wondered how long hacking would take to pay back the $1.47 million.

"It doesn't have to end, Waldo."

"Good. Good. It wasn't my fault. I didn't really know how big the overdraft was, you know. You go from fourteen hundred dollars to say a million and you sort of lose track. Kind of. Know what I mean? It gets away from you. For God's sake, have mercy on me. Please. I confess. I did it. Please."

Waldo was crying. He was on his knees.

"I'll do anything. Anything. I'll hack in Harlem. I'll pick up blacks on street corners at three A.M. Anything."

"Very good, Waldo," said the sinuous voice. "Although to be truthful, I wish you had shown some more resistance."

"Sure. I'll resist. What should I do? Don't send me to jail."

"Just reach under the chair," the voice said.

"With my hand?"

"With your hand."

He couldn't get his hand underneath the wooden chair fast enough. He picked up a splinter under his thumbnail, he reached so hard. There was a picture taped under the chair and he tore it out so quickly he ripped a small corner of it.

The picture was of a pretty young woman with a blond perky face, perhaps in her early twenties.

"That is Pamela Thrushwell. She is twenty-four, over here from England. She works at the International Computer Advancement Center of New York. You can call it the computer center."

"I've never killed anybody," Waldo said.

"Please don't jump to conclusions."

"Don't worry. Whatever it is, I'll do it," Waldo said.

"Good, because you'll like it. Do you think she's beautiful?"

"Yes."

"Listen carefully then. You will go to the computer center in downtown Manhattan and find Pamela Thrushwell and walk up to her and cop a feel."

"Excuse me. I thought you said I should cop a feel."

"I did," the voice said.

"Hey, c'mon," Waldo said. "What is this? What

kind of game is this?" Waldo felt he could be outraged now that the voice had asked for such a thing.

"You don't have to do it, Waldo. No one is forcing you."

"I want to cooperate."

"I would hope so; $1.47 million is an awful lot of money."

"Do you have something reasonable?" Waldo said.

"I would say that a million and a half smackers for a feel is more than reasonable, Waldo. I don't have time. Do what you're told or the police get called in."

"Which breast?" asked Waldo.

"Either."

Waldo put the photo in his pocket. He wasn't sure if he should go into the computer center, reach out and do the job, or if he should take her out to dinner, soft lights, perhaps a necklace, maybe some kissing first, and then let his hand slide down ever so gently until he had breast in hand, duty done, back home to the Park Avenue penthouse and the good life.

Pamela Thrushwell decided the method for him. If he wished assistance on the complexities of the new mega-frame, mini-byte work analyzer and reach-space mode, Pamela Thrushwell would be happy to oblige. But she was not, thank you, there for dates, pleasantries, or to be picked up by perfect strangers.

Thank you again, Mr. Hammersmith. No, and no, thank you very much.

"You won't go out with me?"

"No."

"Then can I just cop a feel?"

"I beg your pardon."

"Just a little feel. I'll give you a thousand dollars."

"The nerve. Bugger off, Jack. That's cheek for you,"

said Ms. Thrushwell with a British accent so hard it could sharpen knives.

"Five thousand."

"I'm calling the police."

Waldo Hammersmith shut his eyes, reached out blindly until he had something soft in his hand, gave a squeeze, then ran out of the center with people yelling after him.

His coat flapped in the breeze behind him. His legs, unused to much more than climbing into bed or walking to his limousine, strained to keep the body moving. It was like a dream. His legs felt as if they were running but his body didn't seem to be moving.

Waldo was collared on a busy New York street in front of a crowd of people whose dreary days were always improved by the humiliation of another. He was really collared. The detective grabbed him by his expensive suit jacket and marched him back into the center like a child being forcibly returned home for dinner. Pamela Thrushwell's pale Britannic features were flushed red with shock.

"Is this the man?" the detective asked her.

Waldo tried to look at the ceiling. The floor. Anywhere but at Ms. Thrushwell. If he could have, he would have pretended that he didn't know himself.

"Is this the man who tried to cop a feel?" the policeman repeated.

Waldo would gladly have faced death instead of this humiliation. Why hadn't the voice asked him to rob a store? He could be arrested for armed robbery without too much shame. But copping a feel? Even the phrase was humiliating. Waldo Hammersmith committing a crime to finagle a fondle. His soul was shredded there in front of the growing crowd. He looked up to the ceiling, feeling unworthy even to pray. He saw television monitor cameras focusing on Pamela Thrushwell's desk. Even the monitors were hanging around. They didn't move to other parts of the center. Their unblinking eyes stayed focused on Waldo and he wanted to yell at them to do their job and cover the entire floor space.

"I really do wish you would just get him out of here," Pamela said.

'It's not that easy," the detective said. "Are you charging him or do I let him go?"

"Can't you just get him out of here?" She glanced at all the people clustered around her desk. "This is so embarrassing."

"Listen, lady, the guy copped a feel. Which tit did he grab?"

Waldo looked down. Pamela covered her eyes with her hands. "Will you get out of here?" she gasped.

"Did he grab this one?" the detective said. Like testing a tomato for ripeness, he put his large hairy hand on Miss Thrushwell's left breast.

She slapped it away and demanded to see his badge.

"If you *are* a policeman, I have a right to ask you to remove a customer from our premises."

"On what grounds?" the detective asked.

"Disturbing the peace."

"Listen, lady, don't get so damned uppity. When you have to testify in open court, you'll have to answer these questions. Probably the jury'll want to see your knockers anyway, to see if there was any injury. So the guy grabbed you. Did you encourage him?"

"I most certainly did not."

"Did you grab him first?"

"I have heard about police embarrassing women over such things," she said coldly, "but this is ridiculous."

"Listen, I nailed this molester in the street. Are you going to charge him or not? What do you want, lady?"

There was silence in the large chrome-and-fluorescent computer center. Waldo heard someone in the back of the crowd ask what he had done.

"Tried to grab that young woman right out in front of everybody. Copped a feel."

"He sure picked the right one."

Pamela stood up at her desk, smoothed her skirt. Her blazing eyes bore into Waldo Hammersmith.

"Sir, if you leave of your own accord and promise not to return, I will not press charges," she said.

Waldo looked to the detective.

"Let's go," the detective said. He left the center with Waldo, but when Waldo tried to walk away, the detective strode with him down the street.

"Are you in trouble?" he asked. His voice was steady and concerned.

"No. I just tried to . . . uh, do that thing," Waldo said.

"You don't look like the sort," the detective said.

"Thank you," said Waldo. He hung his head in shame.

"Somebody make you do it?"

"No, no. Gee, who would do that? I mean who would want me to do something so silly, right?"

The detective shrugged. He reached into his hip pocket and took out a card. "If you're in any trouble, you call me." The embossed card bore the detective's name. Detective Lieutenant Joseph Casey.

"I'm Joe Casey. You've got my home phone. You've got my department phone. If you need help, call."

"I'm all right, thank you."

"That's what everybody says when they're in over their heads," said Detective Lieutenant Joe Casey. He offered a warm hand. Waldo shook it.

He put the card inside his vest pocket and then, carefully at home, away from the vision of the new butler, he hid the card in a small ivory box. On his next Insta-Charge, he received another computer message. This time he was to appear at a different address.

It was another empty room in another vacant office in midtown Manhattan. This time, the voice in the room said:

"Goose Ms. Thrushwell."

Waldo remembered the humiliation. Remembered wanting to die.

He sat in the dark, smoking Havana cigars, thinking for a long time. He could get back into the computer center and stick a hand under Pamela Thrushwell's dress. Or he could even follow her and do it on the street or in the subway. Maybe he would get away with it and suffer only mortification.

But what about next time? What would the voice want next time?

He took out a pencil and computed what his life-style would cost. He thought a couple of thousand a week for life would do, but was stunned to find out he was spending twelve thousand dollars a week and that was before food.

No more. He was taking his money and going.

He read the balance on his Insta-Charge statement and wrote a check for seven million dollars.

He went to the bank. The teller asked if he were serious. He said he was. The branch manager came over. He checked with the main office. The main office laughed. Waldo had only fifteen hundred dollars in his account and that was because of the security blanket of his overdraft checking program.

The next morning, Waldo lurked in a doorway outside the computer center. When Pamela arrived for work, he rushed up behind her and stuck his hand quickly underneath her skirt. She screamed. Another woman with a very heavy pocketbook blocked his retreat, a man yelled "masher," but Waldo dropped to his knees and crawled out of the crowd. He glanced back and saw the surveillance cameras inside the computer center pointed out toward the street. He could feel them laughing at him.

A few days later, he got another Insta-Charge statement in the mail. It was an order to show up at another address.

The soft feminine voice in the new office said, "Spank Pamela Thrushwell with a paddle." Waldo knew he would soon be asked to kill. A paddle could kill. He phoned Detective Joe Casey.

They met on a dark Hudson River pier, facing New Jersey. Waldo had picked the spot for its isolation. He was sure that whoever or whatever was behind this could see almost anywhere. He wanted to get away, away from any form of computer, away from any place that had surveillance cameras, but mostly away from all computers. A computer had started all this by changing his monthly statement. And Pamela Thrushwell worked at a computer center. Waldo thought computer and he thought get away.

"I'm in trouble," Waldo told the detective. And he explained how a bank error had led him to live a higher and higher life-style so that now he was dependent on the money. He needed it. But he was afraid of what he might have to do for it.

"I get the feeling that I'm being played with," he said. "I can't cash a check at the bank to get any real cash, but I can still buy anything with my credit card. So all I can get is what I need to live on."

"How much is that?" Casey asked.

"A half a million a year or so," Waldo said.

"Good money," Casey said.

"Where's it leading?" Waldo asked.

"A half million to cop a feel? For a little goose? A spank? Hey, Waldo, I'm a cop. I get paid a lot less for a lot tougher work."

"What are you saying?"

"I'm saying for a half million, I'd paddle the pope," Casey said.

"But where does it end?"

"What do you care?" Casey said.

"What are you saying?" Waldo asked.

"Spank the girl is what I'm saying."

Waldo shook his head. Something deep inside him said no. Enough. Bit by bit, he had been played into losing every little piece of himself. He knew that to go on further was to lose everything. Even going back to Millicent would be preferable. He was getting out.

"No," he said firmly. "I want to turn these people or this thing, whatever it is, in. I've had enough. I've gone far enough. I guess you do have to pay for what you get, and I'll pay whatever I have to pay."

"Are you sure?" asked Detective Casey.

"Yes," said Waldo.

"Tell everything? Littlest details? Everything? You're willing to give up everything?"

Waldo nodded.

"Listen, buddy. As a friend. Why don't you just give the broad a little bump on the bottom and pick up your dough?"

"Dammit, Casey, it's illegal and I'm not doing it anymore. Some things I won't do for money. Even big money."

Detective Lieutenant Joseph Casey withdrew his

.38 Police Special and put it in Waldo Hammersmith's face and shot away a very large segment of it.

Too bad for Waldo, Casey thought. But a person did get used to the big money. It got so that you would even murder to keep the money coming in.

In Nemonthsett, Utah, a lieutenant colonel in charge of a Titan nuclear missile battery bought himself two new Mercedes Benzes and paid for them with a personal check. He earned less than half that much in a year. But the check did not bounce.

He wondered if someday he would have to pay the money back. But he did not wonder too long. He was due at work, due to spend the next eight hours watching over twenty-four missiles that were aimed at Russia, threatening it with the force of millions of tons of TNT.

Chapter Two

His name was Remo and the Iranian sun was cold this winter, colder still because he wore only a thin black T-shirt and chinos.

Someone had told him that the winters in Iran were like those in Montana, and that in ancient times, before Islam had come, the people of the region believed that hell was cold. But then they had left the religion of the Parsi and taken that of the desert, that of the prophet Mohammed who lived where the sun scorched away life on burning sands, and eventually like all religions whose holy men talked first from deserts, they came to believe that hell was hot.

But Remo did not mind the cold of Iran and the men he was watching did not mind the heat of hell because they were all sure they were going straight to heaven when the time came. Heavy woolens covered their backs, and their hands thrust forward to warm near flickering yellow flames and their voices chanted in Parsi.

Guards every few feet looked into the blackness and told themselves that they too were earning heaven, although not as surely as those men who sat around the fire.

Remo could see the guards try to avoid the cold by tightening their bodies, not even knowing that they were attempting to generate heat by straining their muscles under their clothing.

The cold was real, only three degrees above zero and with a wind that tried to tear away all the body's heat, but Remo was not part of that cold.

His breathing was slower than that of the other men, taking in less cold, having to warm less air, a thin reed of human calm that suffered no more than the tall grass around his thighs. He stood so still that a rock this night would attract more attention from a human eye.

Those around the campfire tried to dull their senses and fought the cold. Remo let his senses run free. He could hear the grass strain ever so gently at its roots in the gravelly dust of the soil that had been leached of nutrients for thousands of years. He could feel a sentry tremble, leaning against a dried tree trunk, feel the young man shake in his heavy boots, feel the shaking come through the ground. He could smell the dinners of beef and lemon rotting in the mouths of those who had eaten them just hours before. And from the little fire, he heard the cells in the logs collapse as they puffed into smoke and flame.

The chanting stopped.

"We now speak in English, beloveds," came the voice of the leader. "We dedicate our lives in sacrifice against the Great Satan and for that we must speak the language of the Great Satan. Waiting for us in the United States are a thousand daggers and a thousand hearts ready to enter the gates of paradise."

"A thousand daggers and a thousand hearts," the voices came back.

"We all seek to end our lives to have eternal life. We fear not their bullets or their planes or any device of the Great Satan. Our brothers have gone before and taken many lives of the unbelievers. Now we too will bleed the Great Satan. But our honor is the greatest, because we will bleed its most important blood. Its snake head. Its President. We will show there is nothing safe from the wrath of Allah."

"Allah Akbar," chanted the young men around the flames.

"We will build groups from students and then, like a wave of righteousness, we will carry the bombs that will blow up the Great Satan's head. We will carry them in crowds. We will carry them on street corners. We will make his entire land of Satan a place of his death."

"Allah Akbar," chanted the young men. "God is great."

And then from the darkness of the Iranian night, from the cold sweeping winds, came a voice answering in English.

"God is great but you ragheads aren't."

The young men in the heavy wools looked around. Who had said that?

"This is the major leagues, lamb-breath," came the voice from the darkness again. "No jazzing yourselves up with chants so you can drive trucks into buildings where people are asleep. This is where real men work. In the night. By themselves."

"Who said that?"

The voice ignored the question. Instead, it replied: "Tonight, you will not be allowed to lie to yourself. Tonight, the chanting is over. The Mickey Mouse Ali

Baba nonsense is over. Tonight you're in the majors and you're alone. You and me. Fun, isn't it?''

"Shoot him," yelled the leader. The sentries, numb with cold, saw no one. But they had been ordered to fire. The night crackled with little spurts from Kalishnikov barrels as ignorant farmboys performed the simple act of pulling triggers.

The sharp noise made the following silence seem even deeper and more profound. Now everyone heard the fire, but no one heard the man who had spoken from the dark.

The leader sensed he might be losing the group and he spoke out loudly.

"Cowards hide in the dark. Any fool can talk."

The younger men laughed. The leader knew he had them back. He had sent many men toward their end and he knew that to get a man to drive himself with a load of dynamite into a building, one had to be with him right up until the moment he climbed behind the steering wheel. One had to keep telling him about heaven. One had to help him put the prayer shawl around his shoulders and then one had to give him the kiss that showed that all true believers loved him. And then one had to stand back quickly as he drove away.

The leader had sent many hurtling toward heaven, taking with them the enemies of the Blessed Imam, the Ayatollah.

"Come out of the dark, coward," he called again. "Let us see you." His followers laughed. He told them: "You see, blessed ones. Only those with the kiss of heaven on their lips and Allah in their eyes can measure courage on this earth. You are invincible. You will be victorious."

The followers nodded. At that moment, each felt

that he did not even need the warmth of the fire, so filled was he with the burning passion of righteousness.

"I tell you the voice itself may have been from Satan. And look how powerless it is now. Yet look how frightening it was, coming from the dark."

The young men nodded.

The leader said, "We alone are powerful. Satan only appears powerful, but like the night noise holds no meaning. Satan's power is an illusion, as slender a thing as the infidel's weak yearning for peace. There is but one peace. That is in heaven. On earth, there is another peace and that is the victory of Islam."

"Naaah, I don't think so." It was the voice, but it came from a vision. The vision in this cold night was pale of body, with high cheekbones and dark eyes. It had thick wrists and wore only a short-sleeved shirt and thin trousers. It did not shiver and it did not fear.

It spoke.

"I have very bad news for you kids. I am reality, sent from America without much love."

"Be gone, vision," said the leader.

Remo laughed. He moved into the reach of the fire so that their eyes followed him. Then he reached toward one Iranian fanatic and with a cupped motion of his palm under the chin brought the man back, away from the flames, and into the dark with him.

"See," the leader said. "A vision. Now it is gone."

But everyone heard a small wrenching sound like a pipe cracking inside a bag of water.

"Gone," insisted the leader.

Out of the night toward the campfire came something bouncing. It was a little larger than a soccer ball. It dripped dark liquid in its trail. It had hair.

The young men looked around the fire, then to the leader. They knew now what the sound of cracking

had been. It had been a neck wrenching. The head
had come back to them out of the night.

But even as they looked toward the leader, he moved
back away from the firelight, and then he was gone
into the night with that vision.

Remo could feel the man struggle inside the heavy
coat and he let the coat be a bag that restrained the
man more than protected him. He played the man
beyond the sentries with little slaps, as simply as if
keeping pizza dough spinning overhead.

Away from the campfire and the guards, Remo let
the man down.

"Good evening," he said politely. "I have come with
a message. The White House is off-limits."

"We have no harm against Americans. We have no
harm."

"Lying isn't nice," Remo said. "Liars lose their coats."

He snapped the coat from the man's back, cracking
an arm as he did so. He knew the man had broken an
arm because he was trying to keep warm now with
only one arm.

"Now know one thing. The White House is off-
limits. The President of the United States is off-limits."

The leader nodded.

"Why is it off-limits?" Remo asked patiently.

"Because he is not the Great Satan?" said the Iranian.

"I don't care what goes on under those rags you
wear on your heads. Call him the Greatest Satan if
you want. Hell, you can call him Two-Gun Justice if
you want. But know one thing and keep it warmly in
your mind. You are not going to kill the American
President. Do you know why?"

The man shook his head. Remo took off the man's
shirt.

"Say why. Say why. Say why," said the man, reaching for the shirt.

"Because," said Remo. "That's why." He held out the shirt for a moment and then threw it over the man's shoulders. He added the big wool coat.

"Hear now something else. You do not represent God. You are little men and have been for a thousand years. You have come up, with all your talk of being God's anointed, you have come up against something that has found *your* camp in *your* country, ignored the bullets of *your* guards, and the fearsome cold of *your* winters. That ought to give you pause. Do you know the old legends?"

"Some," said the man. He clutched his coat tightly, hoping it would not be snatched from him again.

"Have you heard of Sinanju?"

"A new American airplane?"

"No. Sinanju is old. Very old."

"The Shah's men?" the Iranian said.

"You're getting warmer," said Remo. "But not the new Shah. The old Shah. A long time ago. Before Mohammed."

"Oh, the old Shahs. Sinanju were the servants of death. But they are all gone. They left long ago. Cyrus. Darius. They are gone with the great emperors."

"Sinanju is still here," said Remo.

"You are Sinanju?"

"So you have heard?" Remo said.

"The old legend tells of the world's greatest assassins who came from Sinanju and they protected the Shahs in olden times. You are Sinanju?"

Remo did not answer. He let the man see that the cold night did not bother Remo's exposed arms. He let the man feel himself lifted by one thin arm. He let the man know the answer in his senses.

"But Sinanju is from the East. You are a Westerner."

"Are you such a fool?" intoned Remo. "Do you not see the cold made harmless to my body? Did you not see the night give up the severed head? Do you not see that one man now holds you aloft? Like a baby?"

"You are Sinanju?" hissed the Iranian.

"You betcha, you wool-covered bum," said Remo. It lacked rhythm but he didn't like this country anyhow and he wanted to get out. He had finally seen this fabled land of Persia and it smelled. They never did get their sewer systems down right.

"Sinanju is back," the leader said. "Will the Shah return?"

"No business of mine," Remo said. "I told you. I don't care what you believe. But you don't attack the American President. You hear? Off-limits. Repeat after me. Off-limits."

"Off-limits."

"You attack other Great Satans, if you want. I don't care. Run around your streets yelling. Run around your own embassies blowing them up. Do whatever you want, but America is a no-no."

"No, no," said the Iranian.

"Good," said Remo. "Every group you talk to now, every group you send out, you give them the warning of Sinanju. The American President is a no-no. And if you don't listen, then Sinanju will be back and we hang heads like blossoms as in the olden days."

"What?"

"Heads like berries," said Remo.

"I don't understand," the leader said.

"Heads like mushrooms," Remo said. "You don't have a legend where we hung heads like mushrooms?"

"Like melons on the ground," said the Iranian leader.

"Right," said Remo. "Right. Melons on the ground,"

and he hung the man upside down for a moment by his boots to let it sink in. Of course the man had remembered it better than Remo had. Remo had generally ignored the tales of Persia before it became Iran because he had generally not wanted to come here. He had been, of course, generally right in that desire. Iran sucked. Old Persia was probably no better. Legends were always better in the telling than in the living.

The leader was returned to the campfire with further instructions.

All during the night, as the young Iranian volunteers snuggled warm in their wools and furs to keep out the cold, they thought of him who needed no clothes. They thought of the voice from the dark. They thought of the head that had been wrenched off the body.

Simple death was one thing. But that which lurked out in the dark was another. They had been trained not to fear death. Thousands of their friends had died in suicide charges during the Iraqi war. Of course, their friends had been yelling and chanting as they raced toward death. But this thing out there was not death in glory for them. It was the night. It knew. It was there. Always there. It came at its own time and it would come for them.

They whispered to themselves that it was the Great Satan and while they had all wanted to fight the Great Satan, it was something else when it really *was* the Great Satan.

In the morning, the leader spoke very softly. It was a whisper over the cold black charcoal to ears that strained to listen. He said that it was not the Great Satan that had ruled the night. It was he who come from the old Shahs, even before Mohammed, he from those who dealt death, with heads rolling like melons on the ground, like the night before.

One of the followers from Quom had heard of those who dealt death that way. But they were from the East, he said. The vision was white.

"Sinanju," the leader said quietly. "The vision is from Sinanju," and he went on to say that there was only one way to escape the vision and that was never to harm or think of harming the American President. They would not be going to America to organize bands of suicide heroes to strike at the head of the snake of the Great Satan. They would strike instead at other Great Satans. Perhaps the neighboring Arabs would be a better target. Beirut was always good for a suicide bomb. Kuwait was a jewel to slaughter whoever might be walking by. And in Ryadh, there were rich Saudis who could be stabbed, beaten and, of course, bombed, in their bedrooms right in Mecca itself, the holiest of places.

The leader looked around the young faces surrounding the burned-out fire. Not a voice called for a renewal of the war against the Great Satan who lived in Washington, D.C.

Out of the blood-red sun on that harsh dry morning came a sound, like whistling.

"Good morning," said the person walking in over the horizon. He was a man but his face was the face of last night's vision. He was smiling and while he wore only a short-sleeved shirt and trousers, he seemed not to notice the cold.

If one of them had started to run, they would all have run. But they sat around the fire unmoving.

"You sweet fellows are going to escort me to Tehran and there you will give me one of your silly plastic flowers, tell me I am going to heaven, and then plunk me on a Pan Am the hell out of here."

It was the best suggestion they had heard all morning. Remo thought it was pretty good too. Especially the part about the hell out of here.

He was in Atlanta by the next sunrise, in the penthouse of the Peachtree Plaza Hotel, trying to remember the tune he had been whistling the day before in the Iranian barrens.

He thought he had done rather well. He liked the mystical part. He had always had trouble with the mystical part, but this time it had all worked.

"Well?" came a squeaky voice from the main room of the suite.

"Went fine," Remo called back. "Like a charm. Everything you said."

He heard a slight expelling of air, and then, "Of course it went well."

"I didn't think it would go that well. The legend part and everything."

Remo entered the living room of the suite. A frail wisp of a man sat in a glittering yellow morning kimono. Frail strands of white hair circled his parchmented Oriental face like a halo. His stringy beard quivered as he spoke.

"I told you what to do," he said. "I was clear. Was I not clear?"

"Oh, yeah," Remo said. "You were clear. But you know, you kept referring to Iran as Persia and talked about the old Shahs and how they honored the House of Sinanju, and, well, you know."

"I may not know, but I am finding out," said Chiun, reigning Master of Sinanju, teacher of Remo, and one who had detected once again that first smoke from the fire of ingratitude.

"You were right," Remo said. "The legends are still there, about Sinanju and the old Shahs. Still there."

"And why wouldn't they still be there?" asked Chiun, his voice flat and cold like the first ice covering of a winter pond.

"Right," said Remo. "Right you are."

. "Very wrong," said Chiun. "Very wrong *you* are. I have given the best years of an assassin's life to the training of a white, and still he is surprised that what I tell him is so. Surprise? Are you surprised when the cold does not cut or the world slows for your eyes? Are you surprised when your hand is one with the force that the universe intended man to have?"

"No, Little Father," Remo said softly.

"And yet the glory of Sinanju, the days when the great House of Assassins was properly honored by civilized nations, surprises you. Persians remember their assassins. Americans remember nothing, especially not gratitude."

"I am very grateful to you, Little Father, for all you have taught me," Remo said.

"You're the worst of whites," said Chiun.

"When it comes to knowing what is, there is no match for you," Remo said. "I have never questioned that. Not once."

"The French are acceptable although they do not wash. The Italians, yes, even Italians are acceptable although their breath is foul. Even the British. But I was cursed with an American student. A hybrid white. And yet I gave without stint or complaint. Your lunatic government contracted for my services and then gave me a thing like you to turn into an assassin. I should have returned home. I would have been justified. I could simply have said this pale piece of pig's ear is much too ugly to allow in my presence and I could have walked away from you and this imbecilic country of yours. But instead I stayed and I trained you. And what do I get? Ingratitude. Surprise that what I say is true."

"All I'm saying," Remo said, "is that the old legends tend to get a bit, well, glorified."

"Of course. How else could one treat the awesome magnificence of the glory of the House of Sinanju?" Chiun asked.

Remo sat down in front of Chiun. The old man turned within his yellow robes. He turned so that he faced away.

"Little Father," Remo said to the back of Chiun's head. "I respect what the House of Sinanju is because I have Sinanju. I am part of it. But the rest of the world doesn't have quite that high opinion of assassins. And that Sinanju was remembered in Iran after centuries was gratifying . . . yeah, gratifying." Remo liked that. He thought he had really come out of that one well.

Chiun was quiet a moment. And then he turned. Remo had done it. He was so surprised that he couldn't quite remember if it were the first time Chiun had ever responded to his reasoning and his apology. He would have to remember how he did it. He felt quite confident and he smiled.

"Did you remember heads like melons on the ground or did you just say fruit?" Chiun asked.

"I got to melons," Remo said.

"You forgot melons," said Chiun, and a bony finger with a long tapering nail came out from the robe and rose toward the ceiling of the penthouse suite of the Peachtree Plaza. Chiun was making a point.

"If you had listened well, you would have remembered the melons. You would have remembered heads littering the fields like melons. You would have performed better. But why should I be listened to? It is impossible to teach someone who thinks he knows everything."

"Of course I don't know everything," Remo protested.

"Well, I do," Chiun said. And on that he contended that Remo should listen to everything in the future, as he should have been listening in the past.

Chiun was not the only problem with the Iran assignment. There was a message waiting for Remo at the desk of the hotel. Aunt Catherine had called. Therefore Remo was to phone the coded number that would automatically scramble from both ends.

It was answered far north in a sanitarium overlooking Long Island Sound. Headquarters.

"Where have you been? Remo, the White House is desperate. We promised them protection for the next crucial month and then you disappear."

"They have it," Remo said. "They have the best protection."

"Remo, the White House had to publicly ring itself with concrete barricades to stop truck bombers. That's an international admission of weakness. But we know there are suicide groups aimed at the President's life. We can't stop them with normal security. We had your assurance that the President would be protected. Where are you?"

"Home, or whatever passes for it this week."

"What about the protection?"

"The President's got the best kind," Remo said.

"He doesn't see you. Where is his protection?"

"Because he can't see it doesn't mean he doesn't have it."

"Please don't get Oriental with me, Remo. We have

a problem here of Iranian suicide squads who have vowed to kill the President."

"Smitty," Remo said patiently. "Don't worry about those things, will you? It's taken care of."

Dr. Harold W. Smith found himself looking at the telephone now when he talked to Remo. If Remo said it was taken care of, it was taken care of, and that was that and Smith wanted to get off the telephone. Keeping a phone line open longer than he had to extended the risk, scrambler or no scrambler, and Smith found himself worrying more and more these days about the security of the secret organization, CURE.

In his years as the head of CURE, Harold W. Smith had grown old. His hands were not as steady nor his movements as quick. Even his mind had dulled somewhat. But what really had grown old was his spirit. He was tired.

Maybe it was because when the organization began, there was so much hope. A secret agency to work outside the Constitution to fight America's enemies. Someday, a crime-free society. It was a grand goal, but it had never been reached. CURE struggled all the time, just to stay even, and when they had added Remo as their enforcement arm, to punish those who somehow the law missed, it was all just more of the same. More treading water. It wasn't progress, just survival, and it had made Smith a tired old man who worried too much.

But in all those years, not once had Remo told Smith something was taken care of when it wasn't.

"All right," Smith said. "I'll tell him."

He put down the telephone and looked through the one-way windows of Folcroft Sanitarium. The Long Island Sound was churning with dark clouds overhead and the winds whipped silly sailboats toward shore where they should have been an hour before. Smith's mouth felt dry and he looked at his hand. It had age spots. Remo's teacher was old, but he never seemed to get any older. And Remo hadn't seemed to age a day. But Smith had. Yet what worried him was not that his body was aging but that his mind was aging faster. He was slipping.

He pulled out a drawer, picked up a small red telephone and waited. He recognized the voice. So would most Americans. It was the voice of the President.

"Sir," said Smith. "Everything has been taken care of."

"Where is he? I haven't seen him."

"It's taken care of. Those concrete barricades against the trucks aren't really necessary now."

"You were supposed to have him here to protect me. I didn't see him," the President said.

"He handled it, sir."

"I know this sounds a bit far-out, but can he make himself invisible?"

"I don't know. He is aware of how people move their eyes, but I really can't say," Smith said.

"And the older one is even better, right?"

The President often asked that question. He liked hearing that there was a man at least eighty years old who was physically superior to Smith's awesome assassin. The President did not even know that the assassin's name was Remo and that his teacher was named Chiun.

"In many respects, the older one is better," Smith said.

"At least eighty, huh?"

"Yes, sir."

"And you say we're safe?"

"You're safe from the truck bombers, the people who'd give up their own lives to get yours."

"Well, all right. That's good enough. Does the older one say it's safe?"

"I don't know if he was involved," Smith said.

"Does he exercise? I exercise. Does he have exercises he does to stay so damned fit?"

"Not like you know of, sir. It's not their muscles they exercise."

"They do the damnedest things. You know, the hardest part of this job is not telling anyone about them."

"Only you and I know," Smith said. "Imagine if it were known that the government employs those two. Imagine if my agency's existence were known."

There was a chuckle at the other end of the phone.

"I can imagine what the press would do with that. They'd bust a blood vessel with the joy of it."

The President hung up and Smith reflected that at least the man in the White House had not changed. He still held no rancor toward a press corps that obviously would like nothing more than to feed on his liver, even if they had to destroy the country to get to it.

Smith replaced the telephone and looked out again at Long Island Sound.

No one had changed. Not Remo, not Chiun, not the President.

Only Smith. The gaunt young man with the lemony face and the impossible job had become a gaunt old man with lemony face and impossible job.

Chapter Three

Abner Buell waited until the last actress and her pushy agent had left the party. They had stayed too late for people who already were going to get his backing in a movie. They had lingered over his new three-dimensional Zylon game, the adult version where the Zylon maiden ran around on the screen unclothed and the Orgmork had an engorging male organ.

The woman player was supposed to get the maiden through the maze of electronic obstacles without losing more clothes, until she was safe in the castle. The male operator of the machine was supposed to get the monster Orgmork to capture the maiden while keeping the sex organ at what was called a point level but was really something much cruder.

The big selling point of the game was that when the monster got the maiden, they would simulate a sexual assault. Right down to the screams.

The children's version of the game just had dismembering, and both the maiden and the Orgmork were clothed. It was the biggest arcade triumph of the month and Abner Buell had been bored with it in two days. He had created it.

He had also created Zonkman, where a flashing mouth ate bluish hamburger to music, and he promptly got the highest score ever. There would be little awards for those pimply-faced youngsters who scored in the zillions on those machines but Abner Buell knew that none of them would ever reach his score.

But as the inventor, the computer genius behind the game, he would never let on that the best of the kids were not even at half the level of his skill. That would ruin the image of the game, that youngsters with bubblegum reeking out of their insides or wherever they reeked, could be the best in the world at these things.

They couldn't be, precisely because they were unformed adolescents. Abner Buell invented the games for them because during those complex constructions, he was momentarily relieved of what had plagued him since he graduated from Harvard summa cum laude at the age of ten.

Boredom. The appalling grayness of the never-ending dullness of life.

At twelve, he had obtained a Ph.D. in mathematics and was thinking of getting another one in English literature when he knew that too would fail to suffice. So he planned and executed a perfect bank robbery and that was exciting for at least twenty minutes, but it wore off as soon as he realized that the police had absolutely no hope of catching him.

He was twenty-three now, could not count all his money, owned seven homes and sat morosely through dinner with what had been described as the most exciting people on the Coast. His Malibu home overlooked what was left of the beach. He drummed his fingers on the silk tablecloth as the agent talked of the wonders of his client. He saw her cast eyes at him and he saw everyone else leave.

He made an obscene remark and the actress thought it was funny. He called her names. She said that excited her. He said she was boring. She had an answer to that. She took off her clothes. She said she had always wanted to play one of his video games in the nude.

"Your agent is here," Abner Buell said.

"He's seen me do nude scenes," the actress said.

"I'll help," the agent said. "You want me to take my clothes off too?" he asked. "I'll take them off. All of them."

"If you both are not out of this house in twenty-one seconds, I will stop the funding for the movie," said Abner Buell. That finally did it.

As soon as the door had shut, a crease of a grin crossed his face. He had the calm unmarked appearance of plastic, the sort of expression models like to affect. Even his brownish hair looked as if it were extruded from some hydrocarbon base. Abner Buell did not mind his looks and did not even think about them. What did they have to do with reality? And the real reality was that Abner Buell was going to be entertained this night. For at least a half-hour.

The late-night party had ended with dawn coming up behind the Rockies. It was nine A.M. in New York City. He turned on a large gray multiscreen television set and dialed a number in New York City.

"Pamela Thrushwell, please," he said when he got the operator at the computer center. Besides having sound, he also had the operator on the screen when she answered. For a moment, he considered using the voice modulator that changed his own voice to that of a sultry woman, but decided against it.

"Not in yet," the operator said.

"Have her call the number."

"What number, sir?"

"She knows," said Buell.

While he was waiting, he pushed computer memory buttons and reviewed his position on the screen. There was the first player. He had been brought in by simple money, become addicted to it, and pushed as far as he could go. Although Buell was pretty sure he could have gotten Waldo Hammersmith to commit a severe bodily assault. But he wasn't sure he could have gotten him to do murder. That was the policeman. The policeman had been relatively cheap and easy.

Abner had organized the game so that he had only a certain amount of money to spread around and he was not allowed to replace it unless he achieved what he called "Superscore," which meant turning a personality completely around. If Buell could accomplish that, then he could increase his money supply for the game by a factor of one hundred.

But staying within the budget was not the biggest aspect of the game. The real trick was not to lose anyone from service. That cost ten thousand penalty points.

Abner Buell set the video machine on review as he waited for the call. There on the screen was stumpy little Waldo Hammersmith in his elegant clothes; Waldo, the supersuspicious taxi driver who had earned Abner Buell a thousand points the moment he didn't question his good fortune.

Then there was nervous Waldo sweating in that empty office. And then came the good part. Pamela Thrushwell being very civil and polite and Waldo

Hammersmith reaching out blindly and grabbing a
breast.

Abner's lips almost parted. "Nice," he said softly.
That had been five thousand plus points for Abner.

Then came the policeman running out and grabbing
Hammersmith. It was so nice that this was in good
color because there was that middle-aged former cabdriver mortified in bright red blushing. That was the
good cosmetics of the game, just like the maiden's
scream in Zylon when she was raped by the Orgmork,
or the music in earlier games.

The scene where Hammersmith wanted to die from
humiliation and Pamela Thrushwell wanted to forget
everything just to end it was no points but an absolute
delight to watch. Buell almost smiled at that one.

The goose itself was good too. Pamela looked as if
she had been rousted by a cattle prod. He ran that one
over again just to see her face. Back and then forward
and then back again. The eyes wide in that round
blond beautiful face.

"Plucky Brit," thought Buell. He ought to have a
game called "Plucky Brit." Maybe a group of five
figures in red uniforms marching around through
jungles, past alligators. Maybe have the alligators di-
gest two and spit out their bones. That would be the
children's version.

Buell saw Detective Casey talking to Hammersmith
and then shooting Hammersmith in the head. He did
not like that. It cost him ten thousand penalty points
for losing a player. He watched the body of the former
cabdriver quiver on the old New York pier as the life
pumped out of it.

An unsolved crime. He shook his head. No points
for an unsolved crime. It was just a saving move.

Points were only given for real achievements. Making little Waldo Hammersmith throw away his working-class skepticism was an achievement. But having Casey kill him was not. Casey was a bad cop who had always been on the take, and making him a bit richer was really just taking him down a path he was already on.

He was annoyed that Casey had cost him ten thousand penalty points and he called up the current screening of him. Sometimes it would not come in or sometimes it would show just a leg or an arm or a ceiling. Abner Buell never knew where Casey would place what he believed was the code box but was really a self-contained video camera whose signal was amplified by satellite and could be sent anywhere in the world.

He had first used Casey when a bank employee noticed a computer error in the Insta-Charge accounts. He called up the scene on the video screen. There was Joe Casey shooting the employee down from a moving car. No points.

He used Casey again when another policeman started to get involved. Shooting from the roof of a building with a telescopic sight. No points.

Abner Buell glanced out at the Pacific in the morning, annoyed with himself. He really wasn't playing this one with skill, when every time he didn't get the people moving right, he killed them. You just didn't do that in a computer game, not even the early version of Zonkman.

An out-of-focus and dark pistol grip came into view on the screen. Casey was carrying the codebox in his pocket again. Abner Buell checked his joystick control. It was working in unison with the code box. Next to the lever was a little red button. He put the button on user mode.

A printed message came onto the screen:

YOU ARE READY TO BLAST.

"What's that?" came a child's voice from the screen.

"That's my pistol and that's my special code box," said Casey. Light came onto the screen. Wire fencing appeared in a corner. Then concrete at the bottom. Casey was in a schoolyard. He might be surrounded by many children.

Buell calculated instantly. There were no points won for children. Then again, he hadn't programmed any points against taking innocent lives. He would do that right now. Abner Buell punched into his game memory five hundred deficit points for every innocent life, double that, one thousand points, for children. He would deduct a thousand points for every innocent child's life lost in this game. He wondered for a brief moment if that was fair to him, or if it was too great a point penalty, but he decided, magnanimously, to let it stand.

Buell pressed talk mode.

"Say, Casey, how many kids are around you now?"

"About ten, codebox," said Casey. Casey always referred to Buell's voice as codebox. That was all he knew of the source anyhow.

"Can you get to some place private?"

"Kids don't know what's going on," Casey said.

"Some place away from people, even kids."

Children's voices could be heard close. They wanted to talk into the box.

"More people across the street," came Casey's voice. "This is rush hour here in the Bronx."

"How many across the street?"

"Twenty," Casey said.

Suddenly a blue flashing light beeped on the adjacent screen in the mosaic of screens on Buell's game wall. Pamela Thrushwell was calling and her face appeared. Buell had to make a fast decision. The Pamela screen was starting to deduct power points for his delay in answering. Everything had to be timed in these things, or it wouldn't really be a challenge. You had to have something you were going after and something that could also destroy you. Leaving play pieces stranded cost the worst kind of points: power points which meant the money he used to play the game.

He made his decision.

Abner Buell pressed the red button on the joystick.

In a New York City schoolyard a continent away, a codebox blew up, taking out the chest of a crooked New York City cop and slaughtering, in a spray of vicious metal fragments, seven children also.

Abner Buell had cost himself seven thousand points. To make that up, he would have to turn somebody completely around and get them to do something they would have sworn they would never do. Otherwise, he would lose badly. It was moving close to a legend appearing on the screen: "Game Over."

"Good morning, Miss Thrushwell."

"Is that you again?" she said. The pictures from the overhead cameras in her office showed clearly on Buell's screen. Pamela Thrushwell's cheeks were beginning to redden with anger. She was signaling another worker. She wrote on a note: "It's him."

The worker read the note and signaled a manager to come over.

"Bit of a bad day that other day, wasn't it?" Buell said. "People trying to cop a feel. Then goosing you on the street."

"You are a filthy pervert," she said.

"Pamela, child, what do you think I want you to do?"

"I think you want dirty filthy things. I think you are sick and need help."

"Pamela, I want you to do something for me."

As Buell watched, the manager handed another note to Pamela. It read: KEEP HIM TALKING.

"Something filthy, I suppose," Pamela said.

"Only if you think so. I want you to do something you would ordinarily never do. Something horrible."

"I don't do horrible things, thank you. I was raised not to."

"You tell me what you think is a horrible thing," Buell said.

"Lots of things are horrible," she said.

Abner Buell pressed Difficulty-A button on his computer keyboard. A name appeared on the screen, followed by "Closest relative in the United States."

"I want you to kill your Aunt Agnes. You live with her, right?" Buell said.

Pamela Thrushwell chuckled. He saw a smile appear on her dimpled face.

"Give me something difficult, will you, Jack?"

"What do you mean?"

"You've never met my Aunt Agnes, have you?"

"Then you will kill her?"

"Of course not. I don't do things like that. Listen, Jack, why don't you do yourself a bit of a favor and go see a headshrinker. It would do you good."

"I want to see you murder your Aunt Agnes. I want you to lick a fire hydrant at noon in Times Square. I want you to fornicate with a wildebeest in St. Peter's Square, I want you to punch the queen, kick the Duke of Edinburgh in the nuts, and throw a pound of warm caramel mousse on Prince Charles and Lady Di."

"Sounds ducky, love," said Pamela. She was laughing. Buell saw her. The tart was laughing. Up on the screen, the mirth was costing Abner Buell points. She was not taking him seriously. She was enjoying it.

A coworker came to her desk and flashed a message. Buell was able to read it. It said: WE GOT HIM.

Abner watched the excitement, saw an office manager appear, and heard someone in the back whisper how the number of the pervert had been traced. Abner waited for the excitement to reach a crescendo.

"Pamela, why are you so happy?" he asked.

"Listen, you bloody nance. We've got you now."

"Have your office manager dial me if you've got me."

"We'll find the line busy because you're on it," she said.

"Dial," Buell said. "Have the office manager dial if you're so smart."

He saw Pamela signal the manager sharply and whisper something. The manager nodded and dialed an adjacent phone. A ready light blinked on Buell's screen seven as soon as the telephone connection was made.

Abner pressed BLAST OFF. The manager's eyes widened as though stretched open by releasing rubber bands. Her mouth opened in agonizing pain and she dropped the phone. Everyone else in the office jumped away and covered their ears. The high-range penetration signal had worked. It gave Buell three hundred points. Better than nothing.

Pamela slammed the phone down and ran to the side of the office manager and Buell disconnected the line.

Little bitch.

He should have the computer center fire her. Buell owned the computer center—although no one knew it—and he could easily do that. He should have done it a long time ago when she first started causing him trouble.

She alone, of all the recipients of Insta-Charge extra money, politely reported an error and wouldn't stop until the bank had admitted the error. That had started an investigation which hadn't stopped until Buell had brought the late Detective Lieutenant Joe Casey onto his payroll.

From that day on, Pamela Thrushwell had been marked by Abner Buell for punishment, but so far she had managed to stay ahead of him. Damned plucky Brit.

But he had always seemed to have trouble with Brits, he reflected. There was that time a year ago when he had gotten into the British government's computers and almost had Her Majesty's government ready to drop out of NATO and sign a friendship treaty with the Soviet Union. But the British had found out at the last minute, started an investigation, and Buell had had to withdraw. He didn't like losing games, but because of the trouble he had caused the British, he didn't call that game a loss. He listed it in his records as a tie. He might return to it one day.

Abner Buell strolled into his bedroom, hopefully to end boredom with a few hours of sleep, but as he lay down in bed, a new game flashed into his mind.

Why was he wasting his time pulling the strings on meaningless little individuals or small nations that didn't amount to anything anyway? There were big things he could do. The biggest.

Nuclear war.

How about the End of the World game?

That was bang with a bang.

He lay in bed for a while thinking about it. Of course, if there was an all-out nuclear war, he would die too. He considered that for a while, then whispered his decision in the darkness of his bedroom.

"So what?" he said softly.

Everybody had to die sometime and nuclear destruction was preferable to being bored to death.

At last a game worthy of his talents.

The targets: the United States and Russia.

The goal: to get one of them to begin World War III.

He fell asleep with a smile on his lips and a warming thought in his heart.

At least if he started World War III, that plucky Brit bitch, Pamela Thrushwell, would get hers too.

Chapter Four

Usually Harold W. Smith gave Remo his assignments by scrambler telephone through a maze of connections and secret numbers that had in the past included Dial-A-Prayer, Off-Track Betting offices in New York City, and a meat-packing plant in Raleigh, North Carolina.

So when Remo got a message at the hotel desk telling him that his Aunt Millie was ill, he was surprised, because the message meant that Remo should stay where he was; Smith was on his way to see him.

When Smith arrived at the Atlanta penthouse that evening, there seemed to be a small chill between Remo and Chiun, although the CURE director couldn't be sure. There often seemed to be some small roiling contention going on between them, but nothing he was ever allowed in on.

On those few occasions when Smith mentioned it, Remo would be blunt and tell him it was none of his business. And Chiun would act as if the only important thing in the world was Smith's happiness, and that any friction between Remo and Chiun was "as

50

nothing." But Chiun's apparent obsequiousness was really wind and smoke. It was even a more impenetrable wall than Remo's "None of your business."

This evening, there was something to do with melons. Chiun was convinced that Remo had forgotten melons and Smith assumed it was Remo's failure to buy them at the store. Although Smith wasn't sure that they even ate melons anymore. They never seemed to eat anything.

Smith opened his thin leather attaché case whose innards were lined with lead to shield against any possible X rays. On a small typewriter keyboard, he punched in a code.

"Your fingers work with grace, O Emperor Smith," said Chiun.

"They're getting old," said Smith.

"Age is wisdom. In a civilized country, age is respected. Age is honored. When the elders tell of their traditions, they are treated with reverence, at least by those who are civilized."

Smith nodded. He assumed that Remo had been failing to revere something. He was not going to ask.

Remo lounged on a sofa wearing a T-shirt, slacks, and loose loafers with no socks. He watched Smith punch in the numbers. Smith had offered him one of those attaché-case computers once and said anyone could learn to use it. It could store information Remo might need, was not vulnerable to penetration because of the coding system, and could be used in conjunction with a telephone to get into the main computer system at Folcroft Sanitarium, where all CURE's records were kept. Smith called it the most modern advance in computer technology. Remo refused it several times. Smith kept offering. Finally, when they met near a river one day in Little Silver,

New Jersey, Remo accepted. He scaled the attaché case like a piece of shale a quarter-mile down the river, where it sank without a trace.

"Why did you do that?" Smith had asked.

"I don't know," Remo had said.

"That's all? You don't know?"

"Right," Remo had said.

Smith stopped offering technological assistance after that.

Smith now closed the top of his attaché case and looked across the room at Remo.

"What we have is a pattern. It's a pattern that has touched on something so frightening that we can't make head or tail of it," he said.

"So what else is new?" Remo asked.

"Any danger to the throne is a great danger," said Chiun. Remo knew that Chiun would automatically make anything Smith said into something of awesome proportions under the theory that in a peaceful kingdom, an assassin would starve. Like present-day lawyers, the Masters of Sinanju had learned through the ages that if the world was not fraught with peril, one had to do some intensive fraughting.

"We are facing a nuclear holocaust," Smith said.

"That's been going on for forty years now," Remo said, "and all we've had are little wars. If anything, the nukes are keeping the peace."

"They might not be now," Smith said. "Somebody seems to be destabilizing things and we're not sure how or why."

"How do you know this?" Remo asked.

"Just computer hints that our equipment has picked up. Somebody trying to get close to nuclear personnel in America and Russia. Someone or something tapping into lines and codes and information storage. It's like a picture made up of dots. No dot means anything by itself, but all together, they make a picture."

"An awesome picture," Chiun agreed amiably.

"What do you want from me?" Remo asked.

"Find out what's going on."

"I hate machines. I'm lost with them. I can't even work those scrambler devices you gave me."

"They were only two buttons," Smith said.

"Right," said Remo. "Two buttons, and I never could remember which was which. I don't need that stuff."

"Remo, the whole world could go up," Smith said.

"Aieee," Chiun wailed. "We face doom together, O Emperor," said Chiun. His long fingernails were symbols of doom, pointing toward the penthouse ceiling.

"I think Chiun grasps what is going on, Remo. This may be the end of the world. We send one investigator and then another and then another and all these people from all these agencies somehow stop working. They get locked out. They get killed. They get bought off. They go insane. It's a monster of a force and we might be already in the middle of a countdown to a war."

"A countdown? That doesn't mean anything. When you need me to stop someone from pressing a button, then call me," Remo said.

"Disaster," intoned Chiun. "Doom of world and empire."

"Remo. Chiun understands this," Smith said.

"Right," said Remo. He turned on his side on the couch so his back was to Smith.

In tones of grave import, Chiun spoke to Remo in Korean:

"Fool, do you not know that every emperor's sneeze is the end of the world? Emperors think only like that. They are like young women to whom all trivia makes the world hang in the balance. The wrong dessert for lunch is the end of the world to an emperor. Remember always. Never tell an emperor the truth. He would not know what to do with it and probably would resent it gravely. Make believe what he says is important."

Remo answered also in the Korean he had learned:

"It's not like that, Chiun. Smith doesn't get alarmed about small things. I just don't care anymore. We're always going to have a big war, every day you hear it, and we never have one."

"Pretend it is important," Chiun responded. "This lunatic is the emperor."

"He's not an emperor," Remo said. "Just because you work for him doesn't make him an emperor. He's a hired hand and he works for the President and I don't believe in lying to him."

"An assassin who will not lie to an emperor is an assassin whose village goes hungry."

"Sinanju isn't going hungry and hasn't been for three centuries," Remo said. Sinanju in North Korea was Chiun's native village. For centuries, its people had been supported by the labors of the Masters of Sinanju, creators of all the martial arts and the world's greatest assassins. Chiun was the latest in the line.

"Sinanju has not gone hungry because it has had Masters of Sinanju who have served it well and faithfully," Chiun snapped in Korean. "You are not dealing with some new two-hundred-year-old country your ancestors just stumbled over. You are defending Sinanju itself."

"Little Father, I've seen Sinanju. It's a mud village. C'mon. The only thing that ever came out of that dump was the assassins who supported it. Every one of those people are lazy incompetent slobs. You wouldn't have trained me if they weren't."

"You have an ungrateful tongue for someone who didn't even remember melons on the ground."

"How long am I going to hear that?"

"Until you remember," said Chiun, and then to Smith, "He understands the gravity of it now."

"I hope you do, Remo, because we don't know where to turn. We have only you."

Remo rolled onto his other side on the couch and released a large sigh. He looked at Smith and said, "Okay. Will you go through it again please?"

Smith described the defense networks of Russia and the United States in terms as simple as those of a children's book. The two nuclear powers had big guns ready to go boom. These were atomic weapons. But they were very dangerous. They could cause a war that would destroy the world, so, unlike swords and guns, these weapons could harm the users themselves. Therefore, the two powers had to have things that prevented the big guns from going boom as well as devices to make them go boom. Triggers and antitriggers.

Now someone was fooling around with the triggers and the antitriggers. Was that clear?

"Sure. Point me to those trigger things and I'll find out who has them and I'll nail them. Okay?" said Remo.

"Well, it's not that simple," Smith said. "It's not like triggers on a gun."

"I didn't think it would be. Nothing with you is ever simple. Where do I go then?"

"There is a computer center in downtown New York City. Somehow it is involved with this thing. Money seems to be coming from there somehow and occasionally it turns up as part of a transmission link that we intercept."

"All right," Remo said disgustedly. "Where's the computer center?"

Smith gave him the address and explained the problem again in terms of a shelf loaded with canned goods that was being held up above the world with very light supports. The supports were designed both to collapse and not to collapse.

"And someone's trying to make the supports not to collapse collapse," Remo said.

"You have it," Smith said.

"Not really," said Remo. "It sounds like a job for Abbott and Costello to me."

"He only jests," said Chiun quickly. "You have no need to hire this Apple and Cosletto. Remo is ready to do your bidding. One who has been trained by the Master of Sinanju need only hear his emperor's desires, and then will deliver them to him."

"Is that right, Remo?"

"How the hell should I know?" Remo said. Remo had lost the address of the computer center. He knew he had put it somewhere. He might have torn it up also. Addresses were like that.

Before he left, Smith asked the exact nature of the defense of the President against the Iranian truck bombers.

"The best defense against an attacker is in the attacker's mind. It is not the real defense but what he thinks is the defense," Remo said.

"I don't understand. We have suicide truck bombers. What sort of danger is death to someone who *wants* to lose his life?"

"How can I explain? You only understand them through what *you* fear. All right. They will kill themselves, but only under certain circumstances, and I've changed the circumstances." He saw blankness on Smith's face and said, "Let me try it this way. Every weapon, for its danger, has a weakness. The sharper the point, the thinner the blade at that point, right?"

"Yes. I think so. What does that have to do with your protection of the President?"

"What makes these people willing to die is also their weakness. You have to get into their beliefs and make them work against them. Do you see?"

"You convinced them it was morally wrong?" Smith asked.

"No. Listen. It may not be popular in some dippy classroom to say it, but life is cheap there. They don't think of a human life with the same respect, let's say, that we do. It's just a fact of life for these people. Hell, they bury half their children before they're eight and if they didn't they couldn't feed them anyhow."

"What are you saying, Remo?"

"I'm saying I scared the shit out of them," Remo said.

"What he is saying, O Emperor," Chiun interjected quickly, "is that you have chosen your assassins wisely because your President is safe from these vermin who dare threaten such a glorious life."

"I guess that means he really does have this protection," said Smith, who had been trying very hard to follow this thing.

"Yeah. Right. He's safe. They're not going to go at him anymore."

"If you say so," Smith said.

"He is as safe as you wish him," said Chiun with a tantalizing smile. The invitation was always there. If Smith should want to become President, all he need

do was say the word and the present occupant of the
White House would just simply cease to exist. Remo
knew that Chiun could still not quite believe, even
after all these years, that Smith was not plotting the
overthrow of the President so he could become President himself. After all, why hire a Master of Sinanju
to do something as foolish as protect a nation? In the
history of Sinanju, nations were things of little import.
It was the emperor who hired and the emperor who
mattered.

"I wish him safe," said Smith, thinking he had
given an order for the protection of his President.

"As you will it," said Chiun, who had heard a quite
different command: "Not yet. I will let you know at
the right moment when the President should be
removed."

"Well," sighed Remo. "Another assignment with no
one understanding anybody."

"We understand ourselves quite well," said Smith,
nodding to Chiun. Chiun nodded back. Some of these
whites could be quite cagey.

Chiun insisted upon accompanying Remo to New
York City because, he said, he had "some business
there."

"Inside America, you are supposed to serve no other,"
said Remo.

"I am not betraying service. There are other projects of intellect in which I am involved."

They were in a New York City hotel room.

Chiun had a wide flat bundle in a manila envelope.
It was about a foot long and nine inches wide. He held
it close to his kimono.

Remo suspected Chiun wanted him to ask about it.
Therefore, he didn't.

"I have treated you better in this than you deserve," said Chiun, holding up the package.

"Is it a book?"

"I should have some affairs that are private," Chiun said.

"Okay," said Remo.

"It's a book," said Chiun.

But Remo didn't ask what kind of book. He had known that Chiun had once attempted to have some Korean poetry published in New York City and had received two rejections. One publisher said they liked the poetry but did not feel it was quite right for their list; the other said that they felt the poetry wasn't quite ready for publication.

Remo never understood how the publishing houses had come to those conclusions since the poetry was in an ancient Korean form used, to Remo's knowledge, only by Chiun himself. Remo might have been the second person in the world to understand it because some of the breathing instructions were in the rhythms of that language. He only found out that the dialect was ancient when a Korean scholar pointed out that it was impossible for anyone to know it because it had been out of use four centuries before Rome was a city.

Chiun was annoyed that Remo did not ask about this new book. He said, "I will never let you read this book because you would not appreciate it. You appreciate so little anyhow."

"I'll read it when we get back," Remo said.

"Never mind," said Chiun.

"I promise. I'll read it."

"I don't want you to," Chiun said. "Your opinion is worthless anyway."

"All right," Remo said.

"I will leave a copy out for you."

Remo left the hotel wanting to take pieces of walls out of buildings. He had gotten himself into having to read one of Chiun's manuscripts. It wasn't so bad that he had promised to read it but he faced little questions for months about what he had read, and a failure to answer any one correctly would be proof to Chiun that Remo did not care.

It hadn't always been like this. There had been times early on when Remo felt free of this feeling, this having to prove that he cared, having to prove that he was good enough, worthy enough to be Chiun's successor. He knew he was worthy enough. He knew he cared. So why did he have to go on proving it all the time?

"Why?" said Remo to a fire hydrant on this chilly day near Times Square, and the fire hydrant, failing to give the correct answer, got a hand down its center splitting it to its base. It gushed up a stream of water between its two iron halves, split like two flower petals.

"My God. That man just split a fire hydrant," said a woman shopper.

"You lie," said Remo.

"Whatever you say," said the woman. This was New York. Who knew? The man might be a member of a new fire-hydrant-splitting cult of killers. Or maybe he was part of a new city task force to determine how well fire hydrants were made by destroying them. "Anything you want," she said.

And Remo, seeing the woman was frightened, said, "I'm sorry."

"You should be," said the woman. He had shown weakness and New Yorkers were trained to attack the weak. "That was a brand-new fire hydrant."

"No, I mean for frightening you."

"It's all right," said the woman. In New York, one did not go around letting people suffocate on their own guilt.

"I don't want to be forgiven," Remo said.

"Go fuck yourself," the woman said, because when all else failed in New York, there was always that.

When he reached the computer center, he was not in the mood for the cheery bright British presence of a woman whose desk plate identified her as Ms. Pamela Thrushwell.

"Are you interested in our new model?" said Pamela. She wore an angora sweater over her ample front and smiled with many long perfect white teeth appearing between very red lips.

"Is it better than the old model?" Remo asked.

"It will satisfy every one of your needs," Pamela said. "Every one." She smiled broadly at that and Remo looked away, bored. He knew he did this to many woman. At first, it was exciting, but now it was just what it really was: an expression that women found him fit and displayed their natural instinct to want to reproduce with the fittest of the species. That was all handsomeness or beauty ever was, an expression of a function as basic as breathing or eating or sleeping. It was how the human race kept going and Remo wasn't interested anymore in keeping the human race going.

"Just sell me a computer. That's all," he said.

"Well, you've got to want it for something," she said.

"All right," Remo said. "Let me think. I want it to start World War III. I want to tap into governments' computer records so I can destroy foreign currency. I want to make banks go broke by giving money away to paupers. I want to detonate nuclear warheads."

"Is that all?" Pamela said.

"And it's got to play Pac-Man," Remo said.

"We'll see what we can do," Pamela said and she took him to a corner where there was a library of programs that could do things from calculating building construction to playing games of shooting things.

In doing her duty, she explained how computers worked. She started at the idea of gates with a simple binary command. There was a yes command and a no command. The "no" closed the gate; the "yes" opened it. Then she was off and running into how these yeses and nos made a computer work and as she delivered this incomprehensible gibberish, she smiled at Remo as if anyone could follow what she was talking about.

Remo let her go on as long as he could stay awake, then he said, "I don't want to balance my checkbook. I don't have a checkbook. I just want to start World War III. Help me with that. What do you have in the way of nuclear devastation?"

Before she could answer, someone called out that she had a telephone call. She picked up the phone on an adjacent desk and began to blush. Remo noticed the television monitors in the ceilings. Their random movement, sweeping the office area, stopped and they focused on Pamela Thrushwell. He glanced at Pamela Thrushwell and saw her reddened face turn from embarrassment to anger and she snapped, "Naff off, you bloody twerp." As she slammed the telephone toward the receiver, Remo felt high-wave vibrations emanating from the telephone. If Pamela had still had the phone next to her ear, her eardrum would have burst.

She did not notice it. She smoothed her skirt, let her flush subside, and returned to Remo, the proper British salesperson.

"Not a friend, I take it," he said.

"Somebody who's been bothering me for months," she said.

"Who is it? Why don't you call the police?"

"I don't know who it is," she said.

"Who runs these cameras?" Remo asked, nodding toward the ceiling.

"No one. They're automatic," she said.

"No, they're not."

"Excuse me, sir, but they are."

"No," Remo said.

"They are our equipment and we know how it works, so if you will kindly pay attention, I will explain again how the simple computer works," she said.

"Those cameras are focused by someone," Remo said. "They're watching you right now."

"That's impossible," said Pamela. She glanced up at the cameras in the ceiling. When she glanced again a few moments later, they were still pointed at her.

Remo said, "This place is obviously set up for something. Can you trace the controls on that monitor?"

"I'm afraid to," Pamela said. "Last week, I traced that telephone caller who keeps bothering me, and our office manager picked up the phone and got broken eardrums. I don't know what to do. I've complained to the police and they say ignore it. But how can you ignore it when somebody has people come right in and grab you and touch and pinch and do all sorts of things? I know that obscene caller is behind it."

"And you don't know who it is," Remo said.

"No, do you?" she asked.

Remo shook his head. "Why don't we find out together?" he said.

"I'm sorry. I don't know you and I don't trust you," she said.

"Who are you going to trust?"

"I don't trust the police," she said.

"I'm the guy who showed you how you're being watched," he said.

"I don't know who to trust at this point. I get phone calls at all hours. The caller seems to know what I'm doing. Strange men come up to me and do stranger things in public. The caller knows. He always knows. I don't trust you. I'm sorry."

Remo leaned close and let her feel his presence. Her blue eyes fluttered.

"I don't need a romantic involvement at this point," she said.

"I was thinking more of raw sex," Remo said.

"Beast," said Pamela Thrushwell, but her eyes sparkled when she said it and her dimples virtually popped in her cheeks.

"Let me show you how to start a nuclear war," she said.

"Sure," Remo said. "And I'll show you how we can both go out in a blaze of glory."

She took Remo into a back room of the computer center. There was a large computer screen and a pimply-faced young man with dilated pupils hung over a keyboard like a ham in a smokehouse, as still as dead meat. But unlike a ham, his fingers moved.

Pamela told him to move over. He did but his fingers stayed in the same position. It took him a good two minutes to realize he was no longer facing the machine. When he did and looked around in bewilderment, Pamela told him to go to lunch.

"Smoke, smoke," he said. "I need smoke."

"Good," she said. "You go get smoke," and when he

left, she explained to Remo that the young man was a "hacker," a self-taught computer expert whose specialty was breaking into other computer networks.

"He's found a way to get into the Defense Department computers," she said.

Remo nodded and she said, "See these numbers? We can call them up whenever we want. The first one tells you it's military and the second that it's the Air Force. The third says Strategic Air Command and the fourth tells you it's a missile base. The fifth tells you Russian activity and the sixth tells you where, which is where we are, in New York City, and the seventh tells what's happened to New York City."

Remo didn't understand but he glanced at the numbers. Numbers five and seven were zeros, which meant the Russians weren't doing anything, he guessed, and that New York City was still in one piece.

"So what good does this all do?" Remo asked.

"Well, we don't have all the controls down yet. You know, we do this stuff as pure research, to find out how far computers can be pushed. But Harold, he's the one who just left, he thinks he'll be able to get into the Air Force and make them fire missiles if he wants them to."

"Let's hope nobody gets him mad," Remo said. "I hope he finds some good smoke out on the street."

The screen suddenly became a jumble of letters and numbers.

"What's going on?" Remo said. He noticed that the fifth number—Russian activity—had jumped to nine.

"Oh, God," said Pamela.

"What's happening?" Remo asked.

"I think the Russians have launched a nuclear attack against us," Pamela said.

The seventh number—the status of New York City—suddenly jumped from zero to nine.

Remo pointed at it. "What's that mean?"

"It means we've all just been destroyed by a nuclear attack," Pamela said.

"It wasn't as bad as I thought it would be," Remo said. "I don't feel anything."

"There's got to be an error here. Nine means complete annihilation," she said.

"So it's wrong," Remo said. "So much for this stupid machine."

The third and fourth numbers on the screen began changing.

"What does that mean?" Remo asked.

"That means the Strategic Air Command has gotten a report of this false attack and they're checking."

The third number returned to zero.

Remo said, "That means they checked it out and there's nothing to worry about."

Pamela nodded. "But look at the fourth number," she said.

It was a nine.

"What does that mean?" Remo said.

"It means that somewhere in the United States there's a missile battery and it believes all of us have been destroyed. It's probably going to fire its missiles at the Russians." She turned from the screen and looked at Remo. "I do believe World War III has begun."

"What a pain in the ass," Remo said.

But Pamela Thrushwell didn't hear him. She thought of Liverpool, her native Liverpool, and the English countryside going up in a nuclear holocaust. She thought of tens of millions of people dying, and then, in what was perhaps an instinctive British reaction to massive warfare, she reached for Remo's pants.

Lieutenant Colonel Armbrewster Naismith had been on duty in his missile bunker since exactly eight A.M. when he had parked one of his two Mercedeses in front of the battery headquarters.

It was about noon when he was asked to destroy everything in Russia east of Moscow and west of Vladivostok. He could do this by turning a key. He would turn one key and his executive officer would turn another separate key, and then he would wait for final approval, and then he would press a button.

"Quite a realistic alert," Naismith said.

"No alert," his executive officer said. "New York has been destroyed. Total annihilation."

"I hope it's not serious," Naismith said.

"Sir?" said the exec.

"Well, we don't know that it's war. We don't know that."

"It's Bravo Red," the exec said. "We've got to key in."

"We don't have to rush into things," Naismith said.

"It calls for an immediate response, sir," the executive officer said. "We have to activate everything."

"I know that, dammit. I'm the commanding officer."

"Then what are you waiting for?"

"I'm not waiting. I want to make sure we give a proper response. All right, New York is gone. That's a tragedy certainly. But is it an act of war? I mean, maybe our response will be a grain embargo. Maybe we won't go to the Olympics. We don't know. We don't run things. So we've lost New York. Lots of countries have lost cities. We don't have to be rash about it. We can always send a stern note of disagreement."

"I think it's gone beyond that, sir," said the executive officer. "I've got my key. I see the command. I see your key. My key is in and I can't turn it until yours turns too, sir."

"I am not here because I run off half cocked," Naismith said stiffly. "I have a responsible position and I intend to perform my duties."

"The command is to key-insert," the exec said.

"I see that."

"Well?"

"I'm doing it. So, I'm doing it."

Lieutenant Colonel Naismith took the key from the chain around his neck and inserted it into the slot. He looked at the green screen. The missile bunker felt crowded now, crowded and hot. New York had been destroyed. Boston had gone up. Atlanta was in flames. Bravo Red flashed again on the screen and began blinking.

Then a new message appeared on the screen.

It warned that if Naismith didn't turn his key immediately, the bunker would be declared in violation of orders. And thus the real horror of military service stared Armbrewster Naismith right square in the face: if America should survive a nuclear war, he would face life without a pension.

And possibly worse.

Naismith wanted to run out of the bunker, get into his Mercedes, and drive away, possibly to an airport, perhaps to his winter condo in the Caribbean.

The code-violation warning blinked again on the screen. The executive officer was about to withdraw his key and code back to SAC headquarters that the bunker was inactive because of personnel problems. Suddenly, Naismith inserted his key and turned.

The missile battery was operational. Naismith smiled weakly. His crew looked up at him from their stations. His executive officer stared suspiciously.

"That was an awful long time, sir."

"I didn't want to rush into things."

"Yes sir," said the exec, but he made a note in his log that the colonel should be given another Psych-Seven, the basic week-long psychological test for missile men to weed out anything but the basic vanilla. "Basic vanilla" was the slang phrase given to the correct character profile for an officer in a missile battery. First, he should not be the kind to panic. Second, he should not be the kind to panic. Third, he should not be the kind to panic.

The other seven requirements were identical. The ideal missile officer was the sort of man who at the end of the world would make sure the front door was locked. They had happy marriages, modest bank accounts, neat homes, a two-year-old American car they repaired themselves, 2.10 children, no drinking or eating problems, and most quit smoking when the surgeon general's report came out.

Of Ambrewster Naismith, it had been said he not only would lock the front door at the end of the world, but would file away the key in case the human race ever got started again.

In brief, he was not someone who would delay arming his missiles for firing. He was not someone who would be trembling while he waited for the command to fire.

He saw his men looking at him.

"Well, it was only New York," he said.

"And Boston and Atlanta," his executive officer said.

"Well, if you're going to nitpick . . ."

Peasants, Naismith thought. He would have been just like them a few months ago, in their cotton or regulation underwear, their regulation shoes, their simple cars, their print-dress wives, and steak-and-corn cookouts. Did any of them appreciate a really significant mousse, a wine with a real nose to it, morning on a Caribbean beach while it was snowing in Dayton, Ohio?

He had once been like them. Your basic vanilla. He had thought he had lived, thought he had lived well and decently, but he had been a fool.

Valerie had taught him that. Valerie with her laughter and champagne and love of life. He knew how to live life now and to seize its precious moments. What were the others? Little breathing machines who would press a button or not press it on command. They were the pilotless drones of the world.

He stared at the screen, ignoring his men. No matter what happened now, he knew he had taken life full and well. He had used that grand accident from Insta-Charge, and no matter what happened now, he was glad of it.

He remembered how his account showed a higher than proper balance. He remembered letting it be, sure that it would be caught. When it wasn't caught the next month, he telephoned the bank to say they had made not only one mistake, but two. They couldn't find the mistake. The money grew. It became a family joke, about how he was going to be a millionaire until some computer chip somewhere got to working correctly.

And then he met Valerie, laughing Valerie, dark-haired Valerie, who loved champagne and afternoons in fine cars and the Caribbean; Valerie, who just happened to have a flat tire and wouldn't accept help from just any airman.

"Look, I don't want to be picked up. I just have a flat tire."

"I'm not the sort who picks up strange women," said Lieutenant Colonel Armbrewster Naismith. "I am willing to help, but I do not pick up strange women."

"You said that so well," she said. She had that mellow California accent as if words just happened to come out along with the sweetness of her voice, taking a ride, so to speak, with the song of her presence.

"I don't like tires," she had said. "I don't like dirty things and I don't like mechanical things."

"Then why are you leaning so close?" he had said. She had worn the sort of perfume you didn't smell but sensed.

"Because I like men who do mechanical things," she said.

Naismith reached for a wrench. He felt something soft. It was too soft for a wrench. It was a thigh. Her name was Valerie and she didn't move her thigh. She didn't move it the first time he asked or the second. He didn't ask a third.

They met in a motel out of the state where his own men wouldn't see him. To keep everything above suspicion, Naismith used some of that computer money as he called it, money that had come into his bank account by a computer accident.

It was going to be a quickie, one passionate affair, remove that overwhelming sudden lust he could not control and then go home to his wife. The only thing quick about it was the time it took.

He started to apologize for being so premature. But Valerie did not mind. Valerie was like that. Beautiful and young, yet understanding in ways the colonel's wife could never comprehend. His wife called his snoring annoying and used earplugs. Valerie called it manly sleep. She was tired of boys and wanted a man. But she didn't like motels. She wanted a romantic weekend in Chicago. She wanted the Pump Room. She wanted the best hotels.

By the end of the month, the colonel had used up almost all the extra money and was thinking of cashing in stocks when his checking account did the miraculous. It came up with enough additional money to cover everything. It was one small step to the pair of matched Mercedeses, the property in the Caribbean, Valerie, and life. Above all, life.

He wanted to resign his Air Force commission but Valerie insisted he keep his job. Coming into the bunker became a torture. Dull men in dull uniforms with dull outlooks. He wanted to fly in the sun and all they wanted was to make sure all systems were functional.

He wanted to smell the grass. Valerie had taught him that. Smelling the grass. The others only used their noses when they smelled wiring burning. They drank beer and ate steak, and corn with butter was a big treat. What did they have to live for? Colonel Naismith asked himself this many times, but most of all, he asked it when the missile battery was alerted and his key was required to activate the system.

And if he didn't need his upcoming pension to add to his funds, he would not have turned it at all.

And then when he did, the screen flashed. It screamed silently:

FINAL. GO. GO. GO. CONFIRM GO. GO. GO.

The war was on.

Naismith had to press in the code to release the button to fire. There were three numbers and he hesitated over the first. The war was on. There was going to be nothing left of large parts of America. Would the battery itself be destroyed? He had sworn an oath. He pressed the first number and then the second and his hand trembled over the third. He felt his stomach jump and his hands were hot. He didn't know fingertips could sweat. He wiped his hands on his trousers.

The system voided because of the delay and he had to press the three numbers again. He pressed the first two. His mouth tasted salty. He thought of life and he thought of Valerie and he thought of the missiles going off. He saw Valerie's face on the screen laughing. He saw her beautiful body. He saw so many things.

When they finally removed him from the bunker, his hand was frozen over the last code key. It was still unpressed. The colonel was taken to the base hospital where his wife and children visited and were told by the base psychiatrist that their father and husband might never come out of his trance. It was, the shrink believed, a shock induced by a conflict so severe, so cruelly mainpulated as to leave a human being the battleground between two powerful opposing ideas. The only way most people could respond was to go into severe shock. Very few ever recovered.

At Strategic Air Command headquarters in the bowels of the Rocky Mountains, the staff was grateful for this psychological horror inflicted on one of their officers. Naismith, by his paralysis on duty, had barely stopped World War III. Somehow, the system had malfunctioned and the battery had been given all the wrong information and all the wrong orders. New

York had not been destroyed; the Russians had fired no missiles; and it was only a stroke of providential luck that America had not obliterated much of Russia.

The Strategic Air Command appointed a committee to find out what had gone wrong.

And in Malibu, on the California coast, Abner Buell gave himself ten-thousand points for Naismith and fifteen thousand for proximity to nuclear war. He was annoyed that the war had not started, but he did not deduct any points for that. He told himself that he had been turning people around and testing systems and next he would test the Russians, and then he would start World War III in his own good time. He decided to do it at night when the flash of nuclear weapons exploding would be more visible.

He cleared the screen of the Nuclear War Game and the computer notified him that he was in a chase.

It came from Pamela Thrushwell. The chaser had noticed the monitors at the New York computer center and the chaser had seemed to track every move the cameras made. The computer had footage of Pamela Thrushwell throwing her ample body at the chaser, who was a young white man with dark hair and eyes and very thick wrists.

Abner Buell, boredom gone for a moment, began to trace the man who was with Pamela Thrushwell. It proved to be even more exciting than he had thought. Fingerprints were picked up from Ms. Thrushwell's desk but there was no evidence that those fingerprints were on file anywhere.

A secret agent was after him, Buell decided. An agent so secret that he had no fingerprints on file anywhere.

Maybe they were working together.

If so, he could reach the man through Pamela Thrushwell.

It might be fun, Buell thought.

So few things were these days. These last few days that were left to the world.

Chapter Five

"Don't you eat?" asked Pamela as she put on her robe and went into the kitchen for a snack.

"No," said Remo. "Tell me again why you couldn't trace that phone number the obscene caller gave you."

"First we tried and the office manager had her ears blown out. Then we tried again and the phone company said there was no such number. There never had been. Why do you care so much?"

"Because I'm with the phone company and we're trying to find out what's going on."

"Is everybody in the phone company as good as you?" she asked.

Good? Remo tried to remember what she was talking about. Good? Oh, sex. Remo hadn't even cared when they coupled in the computer center's back room. He had let his body be used to service her and she had had to notify him when she was done. He was busy thinking. Her sex life must be awful if she rated that as good.

Now he asked her, "The cameras in your office that

always watch when you get one of those calls? You don't know who controls them?"

"You saw me check the circuits this afternoon. They're on random motion. It must have just been a coincidence that they were all aiming at me," Pamela said.

"Not a chance," Remo said. "And that is the final word on the subject from your telephone company. Would we lie to you?"

"Want some tea? Biscuits? Sausages?"

"I wouldn't feed that to a cockroach," said Remo.

"A bit cheeky, aren't you? It's my apartment."

"It's my stomach," said Remo. He was impressed by the apartment, its modern rugs and good view across the East River. He didn't think computer sales-people made so much money from sales. There were three pictures on Pamela's dresser. Her mother, her father, and a young man in uniform. There was also a .25-caliber Beretta hidden inside her scrapbook of home in Liverpool.

"Oh, that?" she said when Remo showed it to her. "I just keep that for protection here. America is so dangerous, you know. Do you think I'm being paranoid?"

"No, not at all. Especially considering that there are four very big men on your windowsill, very big, with strange-colored hair," Remo said.

The window came in like an explosion. The men lumbered through, one reaching Pamela, while the other three leapt on Remo. He tossed the gun away because guns always got in the way. The three men on him smelled of perfume and their hair shone in neon colors. Their faces were painted and they wore black leather jackets and one of them had a chain through his ear. Another used a chain as a belt. Another was swinging an ax wildly.

The first thing Remo tried to do was to avoid catching germs. The second was keeping the dye these people covered themselves with off his body. He did that by wrapping them in the quilted bedspread and then squeezing firmly. The last living one told him where he had gotten his orders. Remo rewrapped the quilt and heard the chains on the bodies jingle. Suddenly, he had an awful thought. He reopened the quilt and their bodies tumbled out but it was too late. Their hair had stained the quilt.

"I'm sorry," he told Pamela, who was having a grand old time beating up on the remaining muscled young man. He had his hair shaved so it looked as if his head were pointed. The point was a deep purple with green beads woven through it.

"Don't touch the hair," Remo called to Pamela. "It comes off."

"Why don't you help me then?" she said, as she swung a metal picture frame at the shaved part of the skull. It made a dent.

"You seem to be doing all right without me," said Remo.

Pamela threw a karate blow at his neck and stunned her attacker for a while. She grabbed an arm, threw the man over her shoulder, and then began kicking his face.

"What are you doing?" Remo asked.

"I'm finishing him, dammit."

"You're getting the stain on your bedroom slippers. Those colors come off, I told you."

"If you were a gentleman, you would help me."

"I never said I was a gentleman. Stay away from the hair. Kick him in the chest."

"He's got chains there."

"Well, kick his groin."

"He's got needles or something there," Pamela said.

"Well then, break his ankles. I don't know."

"What did *you* do?"

"I wrapped them up before I killed them," Remo said.

"What did you wrap them with?"

"A quilt."

"My good quilt?"

"It was the one on the bed," Remo said.

"If that's stained, I'll kill you, Remo."

"I couldn't help it," Remo said, and to make amends he finished off the multicolored brute by sending a chest bone firmly and eternally into a pumping heart which therupon stopped. Aortas did not function with bones sticking into them.

"It's about time," Pamela said. "You could have helped earlier. Good job on those three." She sighed. "Now I guess it's the police and explanations. Paperwork and such. Drat."

"See you around," Remo said.

"You're leaving me with this?"

"Somebody always picks up the bodies," Remo said. "I used to worry about that but I never saw a body left around long enough to cause pollution. I don't know about these four though. They may be the first."

"They're punkers. They think it's attractive, I guess," said Pamela. "Let's go. We'll leave them."

"I go alone," Remo said.

"You're not leaving me. I'm not responsible for your bodies," she said.

"I saved your life," Remo said.

"I would have had them," she said. "Besides, you need me. I know computers. You don't even know what a mode is."

"I don't care what a mode is."

"Well, you've got to know that if you're going to track down these people. You've got to know a lot of things you don't know. Or else have someone who does. I am that someone," said Pamela, pointing to a large left breast.

"What's it to you anyway?" Remo asked.

"I beg your pardon. These four lunatics come in here to kill me. I saw our office manager have her eardrums shattered. I have been subjected to abuse, teasing, and general mistreatment by a voice on a phone. I want whoever it is. I want that person real bad."

She had already slipped out of her robe and pulled a dress over her head. She picked up the pistol from the floor and tucked it into the waistband of her dress and did it so expertly that it did not show.

"What are you going to do with that?" said Remo, pointed to the gun.

"When I find them I am going to shoot off their gonads. Now you know. Are you happy?"

"Suppose they're women?" Remo said.

"There are other places to shoot them," said Pamela Thrushwell.

But when they got to the address that the dying punker had given Remo, Pamela uttered a little moan.

"I thought so. They've beaten us again."

"This is the place," Remo said. "He wasn't lying."

Remo looked around. There was no one on the corner. It was two A.M. on a filthy empty street where even muggers were afraid to venture out. Policemen rode two to a car with guns cocked and ready on their laps.

Behind them was a small branch bank. It was closed for the night and the only sound in the garment district was the sewer rats scurrying from one garbage bin to the other.

"He told me his contact was always ready for him. Always. I assumed it meant twenty-four hours a day," Remo said.

"He's beaten us again," Pamela said disconsolately.

"How do you know it's a he? I only have a number for him. Two-forty-two. How do you know that 242 is a he?"

"Until we see her, it's a him," Pamela said. She started to say more, then stopped. She looked to Remo excitedly. "He's here." She nodded toward the bank.

Remo looked inside and sensed nothing alive. This was not altogether unusual because sometimes when it was filled with bank employees, he got the same sensation.

"Where?" said Remo.

Pamela nodded again, this time toward the automatic card machine, a gray metal box set into the stone of the building front.

"Punch in that number," she said. "Go ahead."

Remo punched in 2-4-2. The screen lit up. Bright green numbers appeared on a gray background. The numbers blinked for a moment and were replaced by letters. It was a message:

"CONGRATULATIONS ON A SUCCESSFUL ASSIGNMENT. PLEASE TELL ME HOW WELL YOU DID."

"Go ahead." Pamela nudged Remo.

"We killed the man and the woman," Remo said.

The screen printed out:

"ARE YOU SURE?"

"Sure. He died well," Remo said. "The woman made a lot of noise."

"WHAT KIND OF NOISE?" the screen printed.

"Good noise," said Remo. He looked to Pamela and shrugged. What was he supposed to say?

"YOU LIE," said the machine.

"How do you know?"

"BECAUSE I CAN SEE YOU. I CAN SEE YOU AND THAT BIG-TITTED BRIT TROUBLEMAKER. TELL HER I WANT HER TO LICK THAT FIRE HYDRANT."

"Take a hike," Remo said.

"WHO ARE YOU? I CANNOT FIND OUT WHO YOU ARE."

"You're not supposed to," Remo said.

The machine's cash drawer opened. A stack of hundred-dollar bills an inch high appeared.

"What's this for?" Remo asked.

"FOR YOU. WHO ARE YOU?"

Remo took the money and slammed it back into the cash drawer, then shoved the drawer shut.

"WHAT DO YOU WANT?" came the printed message.

"To destroy you," Remo said. "I am coming to kill you."

The machine blinked again as though in some sort of joy and flashed out an insane jumble of letters and numbers. Then it flashed again in capitals:

"CONGRATULATIONS, WHOEVER YOU ARE. YOU ARE WORTH 50,000 POINTS."

The machine went dead dark in the night.

"It's gone. Bugger it, it's gone," Pamela said.

"Maybe we can trace it," Remo said.

"I hope so, I want to shoot his nougats off," said Pamela.

"You're a vicious little thing, aren't you?"

"I didn't bash in those three blokes at my flat, you know. And with my good spread, too. You did. You're violent. That's because you're an American. I'm British. I only do what is necessary to keep a bit of order in this world."

"Well, order this for a while," Remo said. "Figure out how we can find out who's using this bank's computer system."

"We can't," she said.

"Why not?"

"Because it's at the bank's main headquarters down on Wall Street. And the information storage is shielded behind steel doors that can't be opened by outsiders and can't be penetrated by another computer."

"But people can get into it," Remo said.

"They have guards and guns and walls and gates and things. Really, it's impossible."

"Yeah, yeah," Remo said. "You coming?"

"You want me now?" said Pamela.

"I've got to have someone who tells me what we'll find. If we get in to that computer thingamajig, can we get to whoever's behind this?"

"We've got a chance," Pamela said.

"Then let's go."

There was little trouble getting through the guards and rounding up the people who had the right combinations and keys to the secret computer files. Remo merely had to wake them up and tell them they were needed. He did this by holding them out of their apartment windows by their ankles. They were, of course, all vice-presidents of the bank.

"Listen," Remo said. "You and I have a problem. You don't want to see the street coming up at you and I don't want to spend the night waiting outside your main storage vault. Can we come to some mutual understanding?"

"Yes," agreed all five vice-presidents, they could. Negotiation was always preferable to confrontation. The one who did not wish to negotiate lived on the ground floor. But when it was explained to him that he could be worked into the concrete, facefirst, with the same amount of force as in a twenty-story fall, he

too decided to join the management team that was
going to open the main vault's computer section.

All five appeared in their underwear at 5:10 A.M. at
the main vault, telling the guard to open up.

"Is something wrong?" asked the guard.

"No," said Remo. "We're having a pajama party."

Chapter Six

Western intelligence sources had determined there were five major missile units inside the Soviet Union, whose sights were aimed at the United States. This was because the Central Intelligence Agency had more faith in Russian technological competence than did the Kremlin.

The Kremlin actually had twenty main missile units, and three dozen secondary launch units. They had this many because, unlike peace activists, the Kremlin planners did not imagine their missiles landing dead center in whatever city some peace activist was talking in.

The Kremlin knew that war was a system of vagaries and things that go wrong. They knew it was the remnants of armies that won wars, not the armies a nation began the war with. Communism had given them a system far in advance of the West: through Communism, they already knew nothing worked; the West was still finding it out.

In their twenty main missile batteries were the most massive nuclear warheads available, each capable of destroying half of America. Enough nuclear firepower was aimed at the United States to irradiate America 279 times.

What the Kremlin hoped for was a good hit or two and then keep firing.

The Kremlin did not have people marching in the street telling the leaders to get rid of their arms. They did, however, have people marching in the streets. They marched in rows, carrying banners. The banners told Russia's leaders to build peace through strength. The banners were usually shown in parades, being carried right in front of the mobile nuclear missiles, and right after them.

No one was foolish enough to protest a Soviet missile, no matter where it was located. The missile protests began on the other side of the Berlin Wall and when Russia could move that wall westward—perhaps to France—then all the protests about missiles in West Germany would stop. They would stop because the protesters would realize that being next door to a missile or having one in your backyard was better than being shot, hanged, or jailed.

The onetime protestors of Western missiles would then become part of the truly peaceful peace movement of the Soviet bloc. They would line up peacefully where told, march peacefully where told, stop marching peacefully when told, and then go peacefully home when told, usually to get blind drunk and urinate in the living room.

This was the typical march of the typical Russian peace activist. Sometimes, American ministers and peace activists were along the route of march and waved at them. One peace activist kept bothering the marchers, saying he wanted to "get to know the real Russian, to understand my Russian brother."

But he made a small mistake. The real Russian he was to get to know hadn't shown up on time and another real Russian he was to get to know had to be found quickly, and barely had time to memorize all his answers at KGB headquarters, where these real Russians were trained and then turned loose to let themselves be hugged by American ministers who would then return home to write newspaper columns on the Real Russia, insinuating that news reports of Russian life were misleading.

It was one of the better jobs in the Soviet Union, being a "real Russian" for American clergymen or, for the equally predecided, the average British journalist. Although the British journalists were even easier: they didn't need "real Russians" to give them the Real Russian story. They had already learned that back in Britain from their Marxist professors. For the British, a Real Russian didn't even have to avoid urinating on the living-room floor. For when a British journalist was practicing realism, nothing could bring him out of his trance. Not even soggy feet.

Average Russians, the men in the street, were never allowed near a missile battery. Not only did the Russians not have to face protests about where they located missile bases, if they did not like the town a battery was to serve in, they removed it. The town, that is.

Each missile battery had its own food supplies for a half year, stores, schools, and hospital. Each battery was like a little city, commanded by a full field marshal.

Each field marshal had the highest perks available to any Communist in Russia. Each field marshal lived like a little capitalist and there was no way to reach one with any material goods because he lived like an an upper-middle-class American.

Only the lowest-ranking privates ate Russian food or used Russian goods and then only as a strict punishment. It was the only punishment available because they could not be sent to Siberia, since they already were in Siberia. Discipline therefore was very good at those bases, they being the last bastion in the world where an American car or machine was thought of as superior.

They even had American video games.

And that was how Abner Buell decided he could infiltrate the Russian missile command and have them ready to start World War III when he decided he was bored enough and it was time to end the world.

Marshal Ivan Michenko considered himself a ladies' man and a superior chess player. He considered life a game and his rise to field marshal in the Soviet Missile Command a game won. There were few challenges left until he played Zork Avenger and quickly became the best player on the base, even when his subordinates were really trying, even when he had a quart of vodka in his belly and a woman on his lap.

Michenko got a monthly score sheet, available to the highest-ranking Russians, so that they could compare their scores in Zork Avenger, Eat-Man, and Missile Attack against other players.

Marshal Michenko's were always the second highest scores in the world. He was second in Zork Avenger, second in Eat-Man, and when it came to Missile Attack, he was, to his shock and shame, second in that also. He was second in all three games to a player known simply as AB.

Michenko was sure that AB either cheated or did not exist, that an impossibly high score had been set up in these games so that a Russian could not win. He let the KGB know about his suspicions. He let others know that a Russian field marshal had lost at Missile Attack.

"Comrade Michenko, what are you getting at?" he was asked by the KGB officer with whom he was sharing his worries.

"The great danger in this world is to appear weak. Second best in Missile Attack, although admittedly it is but a game, is still just second best. And to whom? An American."

"It is just a game, comrade field marshal."

"I know that and you know that. But who knows what some fools will say?"

"Who cares what fools say?" the KGB officer said.

"If that be the case, then you eliminate the value of the opinion of ninety-nine percent of the world," Michenko said.

Within a day, Field Marshal Michenko got the information he wanted. AB did indeed exist but no one could track him down. However, AB had a standing offer of fifty thousand dollars to anyone who could defeat him at Missile Attack. He had almost as many offers as there were dollars, but AB accepted none, saying they were unworthy of his time.

Michenko issued a challenge but got no response. There the matter lay for months, until one day he was notified that AB would play him.

AB sent a special joystick, one designed for head-to-head combat, to an address in Switzerland. The KGB picked it up.

The first game was conducted by satellite and beamed to a station in Zurich. Michenko, through brilliant conservation of his atomizing power, and concentration of his beam modes, won a magnificent struggle. Barely. AB won the second game as if he had been playing a child. And then came the third game

and soon Michenko was down by 220,000 points, his
time and firepower diminished, and he could do only
one thing. He harnessed the most powerful brain en-
ergy in Russia. He used his American computers that
guided his Russian missiles. He locked them into the
game and he won.

He did not know that across the world, an American who fit the initials AB, Abner Buell, had just
given himself five thousand points.

They played seven more games, sometimes beaming
challenges to each other, sometimes asking personal
questions. During one questioning period, about the
taste of good cognac, a fire order came to Michenko
from Moscow. World War III was on.

Michenko looked at the orders and his stomach felt
as if it were dissolving through his rectum. There
were no countermands, only his American opponent
AB signaling another friendly question.

Michenko made one last check. He telephoned
Moscow. The phone did not answer. Moscow, he
thought, must be destroyed.

He messaged regrets to his American counterpart
and said, "Good-bye."

He could not know that Abner Buell was frantically
trying to call off the Russian attack. Buell had used
the games to work his way into Michenko's computers
and had given them the firing order. He only wanted
the missile command to take the preliminary steps
before being called off by Moscow.

But now he found the Russian equipment was no
longer picking up his command signals.

There was only Michenko's terse good-bye.

Abner Buell had miscalculated. The world was going
to be destroyed—and ahead of schedule too.

"There it goes," said Abner.

"There goes what?" said his date for the evening, an exquisite European redhead who had to learn to look stupid for lipstick ads.

"You'll see," Buell said. He had a lukewarm smile.

The redhead was exuding from a shiny lamé swimsuit.

"What will I see?" she asked.

"Do you like mushrooms?"

"Only to chew, not to eat," she said.

"Good. You're going to be seeing a lot of them over the horizon. Great effects. Multicolored clouds. Sunrises all over."

The redhead inhaled a string of white powder. Abner Buell had the best cocaine on the Coast. He never used it; it bored him.

"You ought to try this. This is mean mother coke," said the model.

"Won't be time for that," Buell said. He was sure they would be able to see the naval base at San Diego go up in an intense orange ball.

In Michenko's missile station, World War III was getting under way. All the buttons went, one after another, triggering other stations in an entire massive Russian response. Automatically, the first and second waves of missiles were ignited, their loads of death primed and ready. Michenko poured flagons of vodka for every man in the station, then pressed the fire button.

He led a toast to Mother Russia. He drank to the people of their great country. He drank to the Communist party. He even drank to the old czars.

Then a sergeant spoke up.

"Shouldn't we have felt the ground shiver from the thrust of the rockets?"

"I don't feel anything," said a lieutenant. "I haven't since the first toast."

"But, comrade lieutenant, I remember when we all fired the practice missile into the Pacific."

"The one that landed in the Antarctic?"

"Yes, comrade officer. The one aimed at the Pacific."

"Yes. I remember."

"Well, the ground shook," the sergeant said.

"Yes, it shook. Our boosters are powerful. Russia is powerful."

"But we just fired all our rockets and we didn't feel one little shake," the sergeant said nervously.

The officer slapped the sergeant.

"Are you saying we failed our duty?"

"No, comrade lieutenant. We never failed our duty. The Jews failed us. The Germans failed us," said the sergeant, referring to the purge from the Missile Command of any Russian who had German or Jewish lineage. They were considered untrustworthy to defend Mother Russia. Only White Russians operated the missile bases.

"That's possible," said the lieutenant.

"They didn't go off," said Marshal Michenko. "They didn't go off."

He attempted to reach Moscow again. There was an answer this time. No, there had been no attack on Moscow, and no, there were no orders to fire missiles. Why? Had any been fired?

Michenko sent officers out to the silos. They peered into each one.

"No. Not one has been fired," Michenko was able to report.

Nor had the other nineteen main bases fired a missile.

The horror of it struck home.

The main wave of Russia's missile defense did not work.

A major strategic decision now faced the leaders in the Kremlin.

When they had shot down the Korean passenger liner over eastern Russia, they had signaled a warning four times to the airplane. Four different radio stations had warned the passenger jet. Unfortunately, the four different stations had used Russian radios and it wasn't until the aircraft had been shot down that the Russian commanders had realized that the Koreans weren't ignoring the commands; they just hadn't received them.

The question then for Russia was whether to admit the weakness of their instruments or to accept the moral outrage of the world. That was a simple question and the Kremlin decided immediately to let the world believe it had coldly blown three hundred civilians from the skies with no provocation.

But this was a harder decision to make.

They could let the missiles sit uselessly in the silos and let the world keep believing that Russia still had the capability of using them.

Or they could fix them. If they fixed them, the Americans might find out something was wrong. If they didn't fix them, the Americans might still find out, and then everyone could kiss foreign policy good-bye.

They decided to fix.

And in the crisis, they needed people totally familiar with the American technology they had stolen. There was only one country to turn to.

The Japanese had three hundred technicians in Moscow by midnight. Not only could they guarantee that the missiles would work, but they were willing to redesign the silos and make construction cheaper and upgrade the nuclear fallout to include such virulent carbon poisons that even plants wouldn't grow in America for two hundred years.

They demanded a fast answer from the Russians, because the leaders of their delegation had to return to Japan to prepare Hiroshima Day, protesting America's use of atomic weapons on Japan to end a war Japan had started.

Before American intelligence found out about the missile failures, the Japanese had the missiles all working better than they ever had and had established four car dealerships in Missile Base Michenko to boot.

The cars, somehow, would be the only ones that worked well in the Siberian winter.

When there were no mushroom clouds and when San Diego remained unlit far down the California coast, Abner Buell realized something had gone wrong. He went to work rechecking his program and found the Russian missile flaws before they did. The weapons had all been designed and set up correctly, but there had been no upkeep on them and in the harsh Siberian winter, their metal parts had corroded. The Russian missile commanders had pressed useless buttons.

The redheaded model whose name was Marcia was still in the house, leaning over his shoulder as he manipulated his computers, and when he told her that the world wasn't going to be destroyed right away, she looked disappointed, and Abner Buell thought he might be in love.

"Why are you disappointed?" he asked.

"Because I wanted to see the explosions and the dead."

"Why?"

"Because everything else is boring."

"You'd be dead too," he said.

"It'd be worth it," she said.

"Take off your clothes," he said.

Later, he tried to decide who he would like to fire the first salvos, America or Russia.

He couldn't make up his mind, and to pass the time, he decided to finish off that New York problem. He was bored with Pamela Thrushwell and that bodyguard she now had, the one whose fingerprints didn't show up anywhere. The one who had refused to take money from the bank machine. Maybe something elemental would be real good, he thought. Maybe a fight to the death.

He turned to Marcia. Her clothes lay on the floor where she had dropped them.

"Would you like to see two people horribly murdered?" he asked.

"More than anything else in the world," she said.

"Good."

In the computer vaults of the Wall Street bank, Pamela Thrushwell had let out two screams. One of them was for the victory in getting into the vaults; the other was for the shock of seeing all the bank records vanishing before her eyes.

Even as she searched for the source of the commands that operated the money machines, the records were being erased. The source was defending itself and taking the bank's entire memory with it.

Two of the vice-presidents were having heart attacks. The others tried climbing over Pamela to get to the keyboard to somehow preserve the records.

"You have backups, don't you?" she asked indignantly.

"That's the backup. Going right now," said a pale and shaking vice-president.

"My God, we're going to have to go back to paper," said another.

"What's that? Paper?" another one asked.

"It's flat stuff like dollar bills but it isn't green and you make marks on it."

"With what?"

"I don't know. Things. Pens, pencils. Wedges."

"How do we know who owns what, though?" another asked, and all the vice-presidents looked accusingly at Remo and Pamela.

Pamela sat in front of a large television monitor as names and numbers flashed by her in a lightning-fast parade on their way to computer oblivion.

There was one final message. It lingered on the screen for a moment.

"ALL RECORDS CLEARED. GOOD NIGHT MALIBU."

And then the machine went blank.

The vice-presidents who were still standing groaned.

"I guess we've really done it," Pamela said.

"Would an apology do?" Remo asked. The three bankers who had been able to withstand myocardial infarctions at seeing an entire banking system disappear in a series of green blips all shook their heads numbly.

"We're ruined," one said. "All ruined. Thousands of people out of jobs. Thousands of people bankrupt. Ruined. All ruined."

"I said I'm sorry," Remo said. "What do you want from me?"

In Strategic Air Command headquarters deep within the Rocky Mountains, a safety report reached its ominous conclusion: nuclear war could not be avoided because someone or something had gotten into the command systems for both Russian and American missiles and was—there was no other way to say it—"playing around."

The President listened to his cabinet discuss the crisis and remained mute. Then he used the red dialless telephone in his bedroom to reach Dr. Harold W. Smith.

"Where do we stand on this ... this ... this thing with the atomic bombs?" he asked.

"We're on it, sir," said Smith. He looked carefully at his left hand. It was numb and could not move. He was still in a state of shock because only minutes before a publishing house in New York City had telephoned him. They asked him to verify a story about Folcroft Sanitarium being the training place of a secret assassin.

Smith had forced himself to chuckle. "This is an insane asylum," he had said. "It sounds like you've been talking to one of the inmates."

"It sounded crazy. People who had been killing others for thousands of years and then coming to America to work to train a secret assassin. Nice old man though. Was he a patient?"

"Might have been," said Smith. "Did he think he was Napoleon?"

"No. Just a Master Assassin."

"We have nine of those," Smith said. "I've got fourteen Napoleons, if that helps. Would you like me to talk to the man?"

"He's gone. Left his manuscript though. It's real exciting."

"Are you going to publish it?" Smith had asked.

"Don't know," said the editor.

"I'd like to read it," said Smith with all the control

he could muster. "Of course, you know we would have to sue if you mentioned our name."

"We thought of that. That's why we phoned."

That was when the left hand went numb. The world was liable to go up in atomic dust and he couldn't reach Remo, who might not have understood the assignment to begin with, and now he couldn't reach Chiun, who might have understood the assignment, but couldn't be bothered with it because he was out trying to peddle his life story.

Chiun's autobiography. And just a few months before, it had been Chiun trying to create a national organization dedicated to "Stamping Out Amateur Assassins."

Either way, CURE would be compromised. The only redeeming thought was that probably no one would be around anymore to care whether one small band of men had tried to save America from slipping away into the darkness of lost civilizations. You couldn't be compromised when there was no one left to know.

Smith looked out over the sound behind his office. Despite the dimming effect of the one-way glass, the world was so incredibly sunny, so alive, so bright. Why did the world have to be so beautiful at this moment? Why did he have to notice it?

Because all he could do was notice. As with everything else. He was sitting atop the most powerful, most sophisticated agency in the history of mankind, served by two assassins who were beyond anything the West had ever produced, and he was helpless. He remembered for a moment about smelling the flowers as you go by. A golfer had told him that once: smell the flowers as you go by.

He hadn't done much of that. Instead, he had dedicated his life to making the flowers safe for others to smell.

Smith massaged his numb hand and arm. He had a pill for that. He had a pill for everything.

His body was going and now the world was going too.

Smith tried one more time to reach Remo or Chiun at all the possible access numbers. All he got was a hotel in New York City and an unanswered ringing telephone in a room.

Smell the flowers. He never liked smelling flowers. He liked succeeding. He liked his country being safe. He liked doing his job. He wouldn't even have flowers in his office. Waste of money. Belonged in a field somewhere. Or a vase.

"Where are you, Chiun?" he muttered. "Where are you, Remo?"

Like a prayer answered, the telephone rang.

"Smitty," Remo said, "I can't make head or tail out of this."

"Out of what? Where are you? Where is Chiun? What's going on?"

Remo simulated a referee's whistle. "Hold it, hold it. Time out. Me first."

"All right," Smith said. "What have you got?"

"We started to get close last night to whoever's messing with the computers and all, and he erased some bank records on me. The last message said 'Good night Malibu.' What do you think that could mean?"

"Malibu as in California?" Smith asked.

"Right. Just 'Good night Malibu.' Any ideas?"

"You think the person behind this might be in Malibu?" Smith asked.

"It's a possibility," Remo said. "I don't know."

"What time was this? What time did it all happen?" Smith asked. "Try to be exact."

"At exactly five-fifty-two A.M." Remo said. "Think you can do anything?"

"I'm going to try."

"Good," Remo said and gave him a New York City telephone number where he could be reached. "Try to get me a lead."

"All right," Smith said. "I'll work on it. Do you know where Chiun is?"

"Probably back at the hotel room. Or in Central Park cleaning up candy wrappers. You never know. Why?"

"Because, Remo . . . because . . . well, dammit, he's trying to publish his autobiography," Smith said, his voice crackling with intensity.

"Let's hope we're all around to read it," Remo said as he hung up.

Chapter Seven

Reigning Master, Glory of the House of Sinanju, Protector of the Village, Holder of the Wisdom, Vessel of Magnificence, Chiun himself had entered the office of the senior editor of Bingham Publishing, then demanded to be escorted out.

"I said 'senior editor,' " said Chiun, disdaining the small cubicle with the manuscripts piled on chairs and the single plastic couch. There was hardly room to stand, let alone to move.

In the time of the first great Master of Sinanju, Wang the Good, when he served one of the greater dynasties of China, a punishment for a minor official was to move him from his office into a cubicle in which one step in any direction would have him nose-first against a wall. Some Confucian scholars took their own lives rather than be humilated in such an office.

"Mr. Chiun," said a pleasant woman with a southern drawl that could smother a sidewalk. "This *is* the senior editor's office."

Chiun looked around once more, very slowly, very obviously.

"If this is the senior editor's office, where do the slaves work?"

"Golly, we are the slaves," laughed the woman and called in several other editors to hear the comment made by this absolutely wonderful old gentleman.

Everyone thought it was funny. Everyone thought the absolutely wonderful old gentleman was funny. Everyone thought the book was absolutely wonderful. The editor most of all. She had some wonderful suggestions for this wonderful manuscript. Just wonderful.

She talked like one of those young women Chiun had seen wearing pompoms. Lots of enthusiasm. There probably had not been so much enthusiasm since Genghis Khan went through his first Western army in less than an hour and thought all Europe was his.

There was even an editor who had cried at the end when she read about the ingratitude of the first white ever to learn Sinanju and how forgiving Chiun was and how much Chiun had endured.

"I have told few," Chiun said in quiet righteousness, content that lo, now after these many years, the full story of the injustices imposed on him by Remo would be shown to the world, so the whole world could see how Chiun would properly forgive Remo. The difficulty in forgiving Remo in the past had always been that Remo so often failed to realize that he had done anything wrong.

Now he would have to know. The history of Sinanju and Chiun's reign would be in print.

The senior editor, her little fists punching in the air, couldn't get over how much she loved this wonderful book. She could hardly go to sleep, she loved it so much. It was wonderful and she had just a few wonderful suggestions.

"Sub Rights has this wonderful idea to increase sales," she said. "Could we make the assassins crazed killers let loose on the world? That would be even more wonderful."

Slowly, Chiun explained that the House of Sinanju had survived precisely because the Masters were not crazed killers.

"Golly," sounded the editor, again punching the air like a cheerleader. "You've got more than fifty assassins and every one of them is nice. There have got to be some bad assassins. Some real rotters. Someone the reader can hate. Do you see?"

"Why?" asked Chiun.

"Because you have too many nice guys. Too many. We don't need all these assassins. Let's have one. One single focus. One assassin and he is crazed. Let's make him a Nazi."

A red pencil flew through the manuscript.

"Now that we have the Nazi murderer, we've got to have the good guy chase him. Let's make him a British detective. Let's have a single focus of place too. What about Great Britain? Let's have something hang in the balance. World War II. Got a Nazi, got to have World War II." The red pencil flew again. "Golly, this is wonderful."

"But Great Britain is not Sinanju," Chiun said.

"We'll call it Sinanju. A sleepy little English village called Sinanju. We're just making the book work better. You can't have more than fifty assassins from generation to generation. Give us a break, Mr. Chiun. I don't want to force my views on you. You can do what you want. It's your book. And it's wonderful."

"Will there be that part about the ingratitude of the white?" Chiun asked.

"Of course. I loved it. We all loved it. Speaking of which, let's get to some love interest. Bipsey Boopenberg in Binding had some problems because there was no strong woman character. So we have Nazi for Sub Rights and we have a woman for Binding. A strong woman. Let's say she's on an island. Along with her crippled husband. And she's not getting along with him. And the Nazi murderer falls in love with her and she realizes she has got to stop him from getting his information to, let's say, Hitler. Why not Hitler? It was the Second World War, right? Gosh, this is wonderful."

"You will leave in the part about the white ingratitude?"

"Absolutely. Now Dudley Sturdley in Accounting had some problems too. He really loved the book. But he didn't like the opening about this Korean fishing village that couldn't support itself so the best capable man went out to hire himself out as an assassin—a tradition there ever since the dawn of history. Let's keep in line with our modern approach. Let's have the Nazi being discovered by a British housewife and then he kills her and that starts the whole book."

"I liked the dawn of history," said Chiun.

"So do I. It's poetic as hell." The fist again punched at the air. "But Accounting said it just doesn't grab. This isn't a poetry book. This is a history of a house of assassins."

"And you will leave in that part the ingratitude of whites?"

"Absolutely," said the senior editor. "Loved it."

"All right," said Chiun with a sigh.

"And let's have a new title. *The History of Sinanju*

certainly isn't a grabber. What about something to do with death?"

"Never. We are not killers. We are assassins."

"Well, you've got Sinanju running through the whole book. Do we have to put it on the cover too? Don't you want the book to sell?"

Chiun thought for a moment.

"All right," he said.

"Do you have a good title?" she asked.

"If it is not Sinanju, I don't care," Chiun said.

"I like something mysterious," the senior editor said. "What about *The Needle's Eye*?"

"Wasn't there a white book by that name?"

"Something like that," she said, "and it sold beautifully. You can't beat success. We've been copying success for years now."

She did not mention that when her company had a chance to buy *Eye of the Needle*, it had turned it down because it wasn't *Gone with the Wind*. It had turned down *Gone with the Wind* because it wasn't *Huckleberry Finn*. It had turned down *Huckleberry Finn* because it wasn't *Ben Hur*.

It had published none of those books, but it had copied them all instantly.

Bingham Publishing produced more books every year that did not make money than any other house in the publishing business. When the annual report came in showing it had lost money, they tried to make up for the deficits by increasing the number of books. This increased the deficits. Someone suggested they publish fewer books. That person was instantly fired for stupidity. Everyone knew the way to show a profit was to publish more and more books, even if they all lost money.

Bingham had once published a fifteen-year-old New

York City telephone directory because the phone company had called it the most well-distributed book of all time.

Bingham put a swastika on the cover, called it *Stranger's Lust Nest*, because sex sold, put four million copies in the stores, and were honestly amazed when 3,999,999 were returned unbought.

"I understand this business," the senior editor told Chiun. "We've got a wonderful book here. All we have to do is make these few wonderful changes."

"And you will leave in white ingratitude for the teachings of Sinanju?" asked Chiun.

"Of course. If it fits."

"If?" said Chiun.

"Well, you know you just can't throw in an Oriental in a Nazi book."

"You have had success with Nazi books?" Chiun asked.

"Actually, no. We haven't. But others have. A lot of success. Wonderful success."

"If you have no success with them, why don't you publish something that is not a Nazi book?" Chiun asked.

"And go against success?" the editor said, shaking her head in amazement. Her red pencil poised over the paper.

Chiun reached a long-nailed hand across the desk and removed, with grace, his manuscript.

"The House of Sinanju is not for sale," he said. And then, with the nails working in vibrating rhythms, he removed the red marks of the white woman.

"Wait a second. We can go along with a few of your ideas if you feel strongly about them."

But Chiun was already on his feet. He knew he already had made too many compromises with this manuscript, the greatest being that it was not written in Hu, the Korean dialect of Ung poetry. No more compromises.

He tucked the manuscript under his arm and was escorted out through the main entrance by a younger woman who told him of her ambition to become a senior editor also. She had one obstacle she had to overcome, however. She kept suggesting that Bingham Publishing buy books that she enjoyed reading.

"And?" asked Chiun.

"They told me to ignore that feeling. If it would bore drying paint and not be believed by anyone over four and treat every sex act like the pivotal point of universal history, then we should buy it. Otherwise, no."

"Did you read *The History of Sinanju?*" Chiun asked.

The young girl nodded. "I loved it. I got to understand something about history and how the human body can be used and how people can rise above themselves if they learn. I couldn't put it down."

"So you wanted to buy it?" Chiun asked.

"No, I voted against buying it. I'm moving up."

"That makes no sense," Chiun said.

"Authors are unreasonable," she said huffily. "You all forget that publishing is a business."

"You really will make a wonderful senior editor," Chiun said. "You will have an office no bigger than one of those telephone places."

"You really think so?" the young woman gushed.

"Without doubt," Chiun said.

"How do you know? Why do you think so?"

"Because you make them look intelligent," Chiun said.

Remo had left a note for Chiun at the hotel. "Be back in a few days if the world is still here."

Chiun held the note in his hand. A rude missive. Typical of Remo.

He went to one of his steamer trunks and took out more long sheets of rice paper and an old-fashioned pen and inkwell.

And as he sat on the floor to write about these latest ingratitudes to the Master of Sinanju, he thought to himself: Maybe a television mini-series. If someone would air that show about that supposed Ninja master who marched around in a ridiculous black costume in broad daylight, thinking that it made him invisible, then they would produce anything. At least that one had had a good title. He wondered if the producers had heard of him. He was sure they had.

"They're on their way," Abner Buell said.

Marcia smiled. The beautiful redhead was wearing a transparent mesh leotard. "Good," she said. "I want to watch them die."

"You will," Buell promised. He really liked this woman.

"And then the whole world?" she said.

"Yes." He liked her a whole lot.

They were very much alike, but in very different ways. Buell had grown up and become a creator and player of games. So had Marcia, but her games involved her body and the clothing she wore, and alone of all the women Buell had ever met, she was able to arouse him. That was the good cake and the icing was that she was just as cruel, just as uncaring of other people, as Buell himself.

"I've got a game for the evening," she said.

"What is it?" Buell asked.

"You'll see," Marcia promised. She dressed and drove with Buell in one of his Mercedes sports cars into Los

Angeles, where they parked the car on a side street near the Sunset Strip.

They stood on a corner of the Boulevard as Marcia looked up and down at the flow of sodden humanity that snarled its way past them.

"What are we waiting for?" Buell asked.

"The right person and the right time," Marcia said.

After a half-hour, she said to him in an excited voice: "This one who's coming."

Buell looked up and saw a man in his early twenties weaving down the street. He had metal hanging from both ears and wore a leather vest over a bare chest. His belt was studded with chrome diamonds. He weaved as he walked and his eyes were half-closed, heavy-lidded, with the look of the alcoholic or the junkie.

"What a swine," Buell said. "What about him?"

"Give him money. A hundred dollars," she said.

When the man reached them, Buell stopped him and said, "Here." He pressed a hundred-dollar bill into his hand.

"It's about time America gave me something," the man snapped, and staggered off without even so much as a thank-you.

Buell turned toward Marcia to see what the next step in the game was, but Marcia had gone. He saw her half a block away. She was talking to a uniformed policeman. He saw Marcia point in his general direction, and suddenly the policeman started running away from her toward Buell.

Marcia trotted after him.

But the policeman ran right past Buell. He drew his gun as he neared the young man in the leather vest.

Marcia said to Buell, "Okay, let's go."

She pulled him away from the corner back toward their car.

"What'd you do?" he said.

"I told that cop that you and I had just been robbed at gunpoint by that degenerate. That he had a loaded gun and threatened to kill us or anyone who stopped him. That he took a hundred dollars off us."

She giggled.

They were at the car door when they heard the shots. One. Two. Three.

Marcia giggled again. "I think he resisted arrest."

They got into the car, drove to the corner and then turned right onto Sunset Boulevard. As they drove past the scene, they saw the policeman standing, gun still drawn, over the dead body of the man Buell had given the hundred dollars to.

"Wonderful," Buell said.

Marcia smiled, basking in his praise.

"What a great game," Buell said.

"I love it," she said. "Can we play again?"

"Tomorrow," he said. "Let's go home now and make love."

"Okay," she said.

"And you can wear a cowboy suit," he said.

"Ride 'em cowboy," she said. And giggled again.

He loved her.

Chapter Eight

His name was Hamuta and he sold guns, but not to everyone. He had a small shop in Paddington, a section of London with neat gardens in front of neat brick homes. It was a quiet neighborhood where no one bothered to ask Mr. Hamuta who his visitors were, even though they were sure they recognized some of them.

Generals and dukes and earls and members of the royal household generally had familiar faces, but while many were curious if that was really so-and-so leaving Mr. Hamuta's shop, no one asked.

One did not buy a rifle or a pistol from Mr. Hamuta by ordering one. First one had tea with Mr. Hamuta, if one could wangle an invitation. If one was of proper birth and proper connections, he might let a few retired officers know he was not averse to an afternoon tea with Mr. Hamuta. Then he would be checked far more thoroughly than candidates for the British Secret Service. Of course that was not saying much. There were stiffer requirements for getting a gas-company credit card than for becoming a spy for British intelligence. But for Mr. Hamuta, one had to be absolutely able to keep one's mouth closed, no matter what one saw. No matter how revolting it was. No matter how much one wanted to cry out: "Mercy. Where is mercy in this world?"

And if one was found acceptable, he would be told a day and a time and then he had to be on time to the second. At the prescribed hour, the door of Mr. Hamuta's shop would be open for exactly fifteen seconds. If one was even a second later than that, he would find the door locked and no one would answer.

In the window of Mr. Hamuta's shop was one white vase which held a fresh white chrysanthemum every day. It sat on black velvet. The shop had no sign and sometimes people wanting to buy flowers would try to enter but they too found the door locked.

Once, some burglars who were sure valuable jewels were inside the shop had broken in. Their bodies were found a month later, decomposed in a garbage dump. Scotland Yard assumed they were the refuse of just another gang rub-out until a forensic scientist examined the skulls. They had been furrowed with small marks like wormholes.

"Say, Ralph," said the scientist to his partner in the morgue. "Do these look like wormholes to you?"

The other pathologist took a magnifying glass to the rear of the skull and peered closely. He wore a breathing mask because the stench of a decomposing human body was perhaps the most noxious smell another human could be exposed to. Coming near a dead body on the rot would leave the stench in one's clothes. It was why pathologists always wore washable polyester suits. Death never came out of wool.

"Too straight," Ralph finally said. "A wormhole

gets into a bone by a burrowing process. It turns. These are more like small nicks."

"Let me see, Ralph."

He handed over the magnifying glass and his partner looked, then nodded. "Like a machine," he said.

"Exactly, except they run into each other. There's no pattern."

"Do you think something was thrown at these skulls?"

"No. Too precise," Ralph said.

"Bullets?"

"Improbable."

"Let's check for lead anyway."

There was no lead, but there was platinum.

A rounded platinum device of some sort had, with incredible precision, nicked the skulls of the victims found in the dump.

They were identified eventually by their teeth, having been provided extensive dental care by the British taxpayer in reward for their having been caught burglarizing British homes and sent safely off to warm jail cells. They were simple criminals, no one got excited about them, and they were buried and forgotten.

But not by those people who made a living breaking into others' homes. They understood the message. One did not enter the simple shop in Paddington with the white chrysanthemum in the window.

Entrance was by invitation only and then only to those who were lucky enough to be considered for a weapon designed by the hands of Mr. Hamuta.

Such as the middle-aged British lord with a friend who turned the handle of the shop door one day and found delightedly that the door actually opened.

"Good luck, what?" he said.

"Perhaps," said his friend, who had already bought

one of Hamuta's weapons. "Hope your stomach is up for it."

"Never had problems with my stomach," the lord harrumphed.

When they shut the door behind them, they heard a dead bolt click like steel ramming into steel. The middle-aged lord wanted to turn and test the door to see if they could get out but his friend quickly shook his head.

A square black lacquered table sat in the middle of the floor with three small pads set around it. The two men took off their hats and when the lord saw his friend kneel down on one of the mats, he did the same. The room was quiet and only dim light filtered in from an overhead skylight. After a while, the lord's knees began to hurt. He looked to his friend. He wanted to stand and stretch but the friend again shook his head.

When the lord thought he would never again get feeling back into his numb legs, a squat man with eyes as black as space entered and knelt at the table. He had white hair that showed age and he stared at the lord who wanted the weapon. His eyes felt as if they could undress the lord's soul.

"So you think you are worthy to kill," said Mr. Hamuta.

"Well, I had planned on purchasing a weapon. I must say I was delighted when you considered me. So to speak. You see?"

"So you think you are worthy to kill?" Hamuta repeated.

The friend nodded for the lord to say yes, but all the lord wanted was a gun. He wasn't sure he wanted to kill anything. He had been thinking of something for the mantelpiece. Expensive, yes, but that was part of the beauty. And maybe in a few years he would take it down for a hunt. Major game, perhaps. But he had not thought of the gun in exactly those terms. More as an ornament.

The friend nodded toward him again, this time with anger and tension on his face.

"Yes, yes," said the lord.

Hamuta clapped his hands. A woman shuffled forward in a black kimono, carrying a tea tray.

When she had finished serving them, Hamuta said, "Would you kill her?"

"I don't know her," the lord said. "There is no reason for me to kill her."

"What if I told you she had served you poison?"

"Did she?"

"Come," said Hamuta with ill-disguised contempt. "I do not have my own wife killed and I do not serve poison. I make weapons, however, that are made to kill, not to hang upon walls. Are you worthy of a Hamuta?"

"I was thinking of a large-caliber—"

"He's worthy to kill," said the friend.

Hamuta smiled and rose. The friend nudged the lord to rise too. The lord could barely stand and he swayed, waiting for the blood to get back to his stinging tingly legs. Both of them hobbled after Hamuta, who led them down three flights of steps, deep beneath the streets of Paddington, deep into British soil.

A large room, almost the length of the main ballroom at Buckingham Palace, was dimly lit by flickering candles. The lord watched smoke rise from the candles. He saw a gentle curve to the right. The air ducts were there.

"So you think you are worthy to kill?" Hamuta said and laughed.

"I think so. Yes, I am," said the lord. Of course he was. Hadn't he dropped an elk in Manitoba three years ago and a rhino in Uganda the year before that? Good shot, too. Right in the neck. Of course if you shot a rhino anywhere else there was a spot of trouble because you couldn't drop him. So, yes. He was absolutely worthy to kill.

"Good," said Hamuta. He clapped his hands again and the woman was there with a small-bore single-shot rifle.

He's not going to ask me to kill the woman, thought the lord. I'm not going to.

"Whom would you kill?" asked Hamuta.

"Well, of course not the woman. Right?"

"Of course not. A woman is unworthy of death by a Hamuta." He put the weapon into the lord's hands. The nobleman had never felt a balance like that, nor such an obvious elegance of precision.

"It's beautiful," he said.

Hamuta nodded. "You are worthy in taste," he said. He clapped his hands again and the woman returned with four bullets on a bed of fresh green azalea leaves. Hamuta took the bullets and cleaned off any moisture. The shells were polished brass and the slugs a shiny substance.

"That's not silver is it?" asked the lord. "Not silver-tipped bullets?"

"Silver is too soft. Lead is even softer. Copper is barely adequate. But for a perfect gun, only platinum is worthy. Are you worthy of it?"

"Yes, by Jove. Yes, I am worthy."

Hamuta nodded.

The lord looked again at the gun in his hands. "It's

a very simple gun," he said. "There's no silver. No engraving."

"It is a weapon, Englishman. Not a teacup," Hamuta said.

The lord nodded, reached into his waistcoat and withdrew a velvet bag which he gave to Hamuta. The gunsmith opened it and emptied the contents into his palm. There were three large rubies and a modest diamond, all perfect gems. Hamuta, it was known, would only take perfect gems. He returned one ruby.

"That is a perfect ruby," said the lord.

"Yes, it is," Hamuta agreed. "But it is too much."

"That's downright decent of you," the lord said.

"Your gun, your bullets. Now you should test it," Hamuta said and the lord nodded.

Hamuta clapped his hands again and a door at the other end of the long hall opened. And there was a poor wretch tied to a stake.

"Kill," said Hamuta.

"I'm not going to kill someone tied to a stake," the lord said. "I'm not an executioner."

"As you wish," said Hamuta. He smiled and took the rifle with a simple motion of one hand and loaded one shot and fired. So fine was the tooling that even without a silencer, the shot sounded like a minor hiss coming out of the barrel. A knot exploded on one of the ropes that held the man. The man squirmed and the ropes fell away. The man let out a shout and Hamuta handed the gun back to the nobleman.

"Oh, gracious," said the lord. The man who had just been set free was large and unshaven and his eyes were flecked with a red madness.

"He has killed before," Hamuta said. "And I think he wants your jewels as well as your life, old chap. Is that how you Englishmen say it? 'Old chap'?" Hamuta

laughed. The lord fumbled a bullet into the rifle and
fired and a little pop appeared in the enraged killer's
belly. But all it made was a little red mark. From his
hunting, the lord knew what was wrong. A platinum
bullet was so hard it would cut through someone like
a fine pick. The shot had to go into the brain or hit a
vital organ, or it would not stop the man.

But the rifle wasn't in his hands anymore. That
vicious beast, Hamuta, had it, and he was laughing.
Loading and firing and laughing. And at this point,
the nobleman saw what he might need a strong stomach for. With one shot, Hamuta crumpled the man's
left ankle, and with another, his right. The poor creature was on his back, screaming in pain, when Hamuta
put a shot into his spine and the legs stopped moving.
It was then that the lord saw the pain and fear in the
victim's eyes.

And there were no more bullets.

The lord turned away his hand and glared angrily
at his friend.

"How could you have brought me to this?"

"You said you wanted a Hamuta."

"I did, but not like this."

"You said you had a strong stomach."

"I did. But I didn't expect this."

The victim's groans mingled with Hamuta's laughter.
The gunmaker was laughing as much at the Englishman
as he was at the bleeding figure on the floor.

"You won't say anything," the friend said.

"How long does this go on?" the nobleman asked.

"Until Mr. Hamuta has had his fill of pleasure."

The lord shook his head. They listened to the screams
for more than fifteen minutes and then Hamuta was
brought a box of platinum bullets and stunned admira-
tion replaced the disgust.

Hamuta worked the bullets like scalpels. First he ended the screaming by faintly grazing the victim's skull, just enough to knock him out.

"I wanted you to hear me," he explained to the lord. "First the skull. Then we take off the Adam's apple. Then the lower lobe off the left ear and then the right ear, and then we move down the body until we are at the kneecaps. Good-bye, kneecaps."

He put two more grazing shots against the skull, then told the lord to finish the kill.

The rifle almost slipped from the nobleman's hands because they were so wet with sweat. He knew his heart was pumping wildly.

Sorry, wretch, he thought, and put a single shot into the heart and ended the whole sorry mess, even while Hamuta continued to giggle.

He did not bother to tell the nobleman that he had actually rushed this sale. He wanted to get to California. A most wonderful target was being arranged for him, but he had been told he must hurry.

"It is a challenge for you, Hamuta," the provider of the target had said.

"I have no challenges," said Hamuta. "Only entertainment."

"Then we will both have fun," said the provider, Abner Buell of the United States, a man who certainly knew how to give people what they wanted.

Chapter Nine

They had all gotten used to the fancy life-style, to the fancy cars and fancy homes and fancy women and fancy vacations, and the fanciest thing of all—being able to buy anything without bothering to ask what it cost.

And then the money had dried up, and Bernie Bondini, checkout clerk who had bought the grocery, and Stash Franko, bank teller who had become a stock manipulator, and Elton Hubble, auto mechanic who now owned two auto dealerships, had spent a month scraping and scrapping to meet their overextended obligations. So when they each received a card that read: "What won't you do to have the money turned back on?" and gave an address and a time in Malibu, they all showed up.

The oceanfront house, jutting out over stone columns, shadowing the sandy beach lapped by the warm Pacific, was a cool three-million-dollar number and just the thing to put them in the right frame of mind to remind them of what they were in danger of losing forever.

They were let into the house wordlessly by a beautiful redhead who silently ushered them to a balcony overlooking the ocean. When she turned to leave, Bondini said, "Miss, what are we supposed to do?"

And the woman replied: "Think about what was on the note you all received."

They thought about it and talked about it. There were things they wouldn't do, not even for money. No. There were certain inflexible rules of morality that they would observe, the things that separated man from beast.

They saw the parade of beautiful beach bunnies walking by on the sand below, looking up at the house hopefully, and finally Hubble forced himself to look away and said sluggishly, "I don't care. There are some things I won't do for money."

"Me neither," said Bondini.

"Such as?" said Franko.

"I wouldn't kill my mother with a stick," Bondini said. "No way. I just wouldn't do that. I don't care about money that much."

Hubble nodded agreement. "That *would* be terrible, I guess. Unless your mother is real old and sick like mine. I mean, sometimes death is a better solution to life's problems than continuing to live."

"But with a stick?" Bondini said. "No way. I won't kill my mother with a stick."

"Maybe a big stick so it'd be fast," Hubble suggested, but Bondini was adamant. "No way," he said.

"Well, I would," said Franko. He was a small man with sandy wiry hair and thirteen months of secret money going into his secret Insta-Charge account had encouraged him to leave his dullard of a wife and disown his two sluggard daughters. "I remember my wife," he said. "I'd kill my mother. I'd kill your mother too. Anything is better than going back to my wife."

"I don't believe it," Bondini said stubbornly. "There's something you wouldn't do. Both of you. There's something you wouldn't do."

Hubble had grown a beard since he had left the grease pit for the manager's office and he stroked it now, thought a moment, and said, "I wouldn't make a porno film." He thought again and added, "With an animal. I wouldn't make a porno film with an animal." He nodded his head up and down once in reaffirmation of this powerful life principle. It was where he drew the line and it made him feel good.

"Some animals are cute," Bondini said.

"No. No way," said Hubble. "No porno film with no animal. What about you, Stash?"

Franko looked up as if surprised that someone would talk to him. Then he looked back out at the ocean and said softly, "I wouldn't screw a dead person."

"Why not?" Bondini said. He sounded honestly surprised at such a modest qualm.

"You never met my wife," Franko said. "It'd be like screwing her again. I couldn't do it."

"Well, you know your wife better than we do," Hubble said. "But I don't think that's all so bad. There are some good-looking dead people. Maybe you'd get a nice one."

Franko shook his head again. "No, that's where I draw the line. No screwing the dead. What do you call that? There's a word for it."

"Yeah," Bondini said, but he couldn't think of it.

"It comes from a word that means dead," Hubble said. "That much I remember."

"What word?" Bondini asked.

"I don't know. It just means dead," Hubble said.

"Corpse," said Bondini. "Maybe it's like corpse-a-phobia."

"That sounds about right," said Franko. "I think that's it. Corpse-a-phobia. I heard that word once."

The beautiful redheaded woman who had let them into the house reappeared on the balcony. She was now naked. Her breasts were full and the nipples uplifted. She wore only high-heeled shoes and they displayed her long dancer's limbs. Her skin was oiled and her suntan flawless, without even bikini lines to mar it.

She asked them what they would like to drink. She licked her lips as she looked at each of them in turn. Her lips were ripe, red, pulpy, her upper lip as full and pouty as her lower lip. And when they gave her their drink orders, she walked quietly away, but even walking was an erotic act as her smooth baby-skin butt swayed lasciviously from side to side.

"Maybe if it was a real big stick," Bondini said. "So I could do it with one big smack."

Hubble was talking to himself, still staring at the door through which the redhead had reentered the house. "Some animals are really cute," he mumbled. "Being prejudiced against animals just because they're animals isn't really worthy of me. A cute animal. What's wrong with that?"

Franko wasn't listening. He was thinking, even though he did not say it, that there certainly were a lot of attractive corpses. Beautiful women who died from overdoses, for instance. You couldn't see anything wrong with them no matter how hard you looked. And if you got them right away, why, hell, they might even still be warm. So they wouldn't give much back, but who said the man always had to be rewarded in lovemaking by a woman's responses? If you wanted noise, later, with the money turned back on, you could hire a woman who was good at making noise. Sometimes you just had to do what's right. A warm pretty corpse sounded okay to him. He certainly liked that idea a lot better than he liked the thought of suffering from corpse-a-phobia.

"I don't have corpse-a-phobia," Franko said. "I never had anything wrong with me in my whole life. Don't go trying to saddle me with diseases I don't have." He looked around accusingly.

Their drinks never came. Instead, Abner Buell walked onto the deck, wearing khaki pants and a khaki shirt which were too khaki to be called a leisure suit. He had on heavy woolen socks, puffed out over the top of cheap sneakers without laces. But his hair was still immaculately plasticked into place.

He stood in front of the three men, looking down at a clipboard he held.

Finally, he looked up and snapped at Bondini. "You. I want you to beat your mother to death."

"One hit with a big stick," Bondini said firmly.

"A small stick. And slowly," Buell said. Without waiting for a response, he looked at Hubble. "You're going to be the star of a sex film. *Making It with Mountain Goats*. You'll have to screw three sheep." Again he waited for no comment but fixed his hard eyes on Stash Franko. "I want you to have intercourse with a headless corpse, dead three weeks."

He let the clipboard lower to his side and looked slowly at each of the men in turn. "I want you to know that I have turned over to the three of you a total of $612,000 in the last twelve months. That's money that technically you took from the bank by fraud. Now you will do what I ask or not only will the money stay cut off but the police will be on your doorstep by nightfall. You have sixty seconds to consider your course of action."

He walked back into the house and when the door closed behind him, Bondini said, "What do you think?" It was more of a plea than a question.

"I don't know," Hubble said. "What do *you* think?"

"I think I don't love my mother a whole lot. I grew up eating liver. How you supposed to love somebody who feeds you liver? A small stick's not so bad."

Hubble said, "I always liked sheep. They're friendly, kind of."

"I can keep my eyes closed," Franko said. "And hold my breath. Corpses. They're all the same in the dark, I always say."

Buell returned in exactly one minute. He stood in front of them, silently waiting. Finally Bondini blurted out, "We'll do it."

"All of you?" Buell asked.

"Yes," Bondini said. "We'll do it. All of us."

"Good," said Buell. "That's ten thousand points each. And now you don't have to."

"What?" asked Hubble.

"You don't have to. I was just testing you," Buell said.

"Oh," said Hubble.

"I want you all to kill a man instead," Buell said.

"Which one?" Franko asked.

"Does it matter?" Buell said.

"No," Franko said. "It doesn't matter."

"Doesn't matter at all," said Bondini.

"Not at all," said Hubble.

All three were relieved that they only had to kill a man. It didn't matter who.

The car was wheezing and the temperature gauge was solidly in the red zone as it came down the snaky road that sliced through the hills and led to the coast at Malibu, so Remo turned off the motor, put the car in neutral, and let it coast.

"What are you doing?" Pamela Thrushwell asked.

"Trying to get there," Remo said. "Be quiet unless you want to walk."

The car picked up speed as it free-wheeled down the canyon's roadside, roaring past little shops that sold pots and hole-in-the-wall markets that featured fourteen varieties of bean sprouts, and past long-in-the-tooth hippies with steel-rimmed glasses and women in their forties who still wore fringed buckskin skirts and soft-soled moccasins. It took one corner on two wheels.

"You're going too fast," Pamela said.

"How do you figure that?" Remo said.

She raised her voice to compete with the whine of the tires and the whistle of wind past the open windows.

"Because the damned auto's going to tip over," she shouted.

"Not if you lean to the left," Remo said.

She forced her body toward the center of the front seat and Remo careened the car through a left-hand turn. For a moment, the car lifted up onto its two right wheels and teetered there precariously. Remo grabbed Pamela's shoulders and pulled her closer to him and the car thumped back down onto all four wheels.

"The next one I can do with my eyes closed," Remo said.

"Please slow down," she said.

"All right," Remo said agreeably. He thumped on the brake. "I don't care if we get there in time to save the world from nuclear destruction."

"What?" she said.

"Nothing," he said.

"You said something about nuclear destruction."

"I was thinking about this car," he said.

"No, you weren't. You were talking about something else."

"I forget," Remo said.

"No, you didn't forget." Pamela folded her arms across her chest. "You just won't tell me. You haven't told me anything since we left New York. You've barely said three words to me the whole trip. I don't even know how you figured out where to go in Malibu."

"Hey, look, I work for the phone company. What do I know from nuclear destruction?" Remo said. "And my office told me where to go and when Mother says go, I go."

"That's another thing. Why is the New York phone company sending you to California to find an obscene caller? Huh? Why is that?"

"It's not really the New York phone company doing it," Remo said.

"No? What is it?"

"It's part of our new phone system. If your phone is broken, you call somebody and if your telephone lines fall down and electrocute the neighbors in their swimming pool, you call somebody else. That's the way we've got it set up now. Well, I'm part of another company. It's part of Alexander Graham Ding-a-Ling. Obscene Callers Patrol Inc. A new corporate setup. You give us enough time, we'll fix it so that America's phone system is as good as Iran's."

"I still don't believe you work for the phone company," she said.

"And I don't believe you came all this way to get revenge on somebody for heavy breathing and copping a feel, so why don't we just drop it?"

"I want to talk," she said.

Remo took his hands off the wheel, put them behind his head, and leaned back in the seat.

"Go ahead then. Talk," he said. "Talk fast. There's a guardrail up there."

She grabbed his hands and put them back on the steering wheel.

"All right," she said. "Drive. Don't talk."

"Thank you," Remo said.

"You're welcome."

Remo had never seen Malibu before and he was disappointed. He had expected mansions with twisting drives and servants' quarters and what he found instead was a string of little houses packed tightly together along the oceanfront highway, their privacy guarded by high wooden fences, and he thought it didn't look much better than Belmar, New Jersey, three thousand miles away on the Atlantic.

Pamela was disappointed too. She said, "I don't see any movie stars."

"They're all out on the beach watching California erode," Remo said.

The house they were looking for was a quantum jump up in quality. It took up a full 150 feet of ocean frontage and was hidden from the roadside by a thick stone wall with a heavy solid iron gate embedded in it. There was a tiny buzzer on the side of the gate and a nameplate that bore no name, only the house's street address.

Remo reached out to ring the buzzer but Pamela grabbed his hand.

"Shouldn't we sneak in or something?" she said.

"Not if we don't have to. Why make work?" Remo said. He pressed the buzzer. There was no answer so he pressed it again.

A voice answered, coming from a small speaker hiding near the gate's top hinge.

"Who is it?" the voice asked.

"What's the owner's name of this place?" Remo asked.

"Mr. Buell," the voice said. "Who wants to know?"

"I do," Remo said.

"Who are you? What do you want?"

"I've come to kill Mr. Buell. Is he in?"

"Go away or I'll call the police," the voice answered.

"Don't be that way," Remo said. "Do you know how long I've been driving to get here?"

"I'm calling the police."

There was a sharp click as the speaker went dead.

"That was wonderful," Pamela said sarcastically. "We're still out on the street and now we're going to have the police for company." She kicked the iron gate in frustration.

"Don't worry about it," Remo said. He grabbed the handle of the locked gate, feeling the warm steel under his skin. Gently, he began to twist the handle back and forth until he could almost hear the hum of the metal as it vibrated under his hand. He speeded the twisting motion and the vibrations grew more rapid. He didn't know how he was doing what he was doing. It was a thing he had learned but it was so long ago that he had forgotten exactly what it was he had learned. But he remembered the result and how to produce it.

When he knew, by feel, that the metal was vibrating at the correct speed, he slapped out with the heel of his other hand at the steel plate just above the gate's lock and the steel plate snapped and fell, lock mechanism included, at his feet. He pushed the gate open with his right pinky.

"How'd you do that?" Pamela said.

"I sent away once for a 'Be a locksmith by mail. Earn Big Money.' This is all I remember from the course," he said. "When I figured out it wasn't going to make me rich, that's when I joined the telephone company."

Inside the house, Bondini put down the microphone and said, "I think he'll be coming in now. Everybody remember what to do?"

Hubble and Franko nodded. They were crouched behind couches with machine guns pointed at the front door. Bondini held a .44 Magnum. They all held the unfamiliar weapons gingerly, as if they might fire at any moment by themselves.

"Okay," Bondini said. "And then when we kill them, we get out of here."

"Right," said Franko.

"Anybody got any problems with that?" Bondini asked.

"Anything's better than screwing a sheep," Hubble said.

Almost three hundred miles away in a mammoth stone house built on a promontory overlooking the Pacific, Abner Buell watched a television monitor and saw the three men with guns in the living room of his Malibu home. Sitting alongside him was Mr. Hamuta.

"I don't really understand," Mr. Hamuta said. "I thought you called me for . . ."

"You will get your chance," Buell said.

"But those three men?"

"You will get your chance," Buell said. He snapped his fingers and Marcia, who had been standing in the corner of the room, rushed forward to refill his cup of mandarin-orange herbal tea. She did it silently, then backed away, never taking her eyes off the television monitor.

Pamela walked toward the front door of the house, her hand extended toward the doorknob, when Remo said, "You really going to do that?"

"Why not? You let everybody know we're here." In her other hand, she held her small revolver. "You think we're going to surprise anybody now?"

"No. But I think they're going to surprise you when you go through that door. Don't you know a trap when you see one?"

"I know that they probably think we've buzzed off," she said.

"Not a chance. They're waiting for us."

"You keep saying 'they,' " she said. "Why they? There was only one voice on the speaker."

"It's they. There's three of them," Remo said.

"How do you know that?" she asked.

"I can hear them."

She put her ear close to the door. "I can't hear anything," she whispered after a moment.

"That has more to do with your hearing than their noise," Remo said. "There's three of them. One of them has asthma or something 'cause he's breathing funny."

Pamela Thrushwell smiled. She knew when she was being joshed. "And the other two?" she asked pleasantly.

"They're breathing normally. For white men, that is. But they're nervous. The breaths are short. I figure that they're carrying weapons and they're not used to them."

"This is all the worst pile of rot I ever heard," Pamela said.

"Have it your own way," Remo said. "You go through the door if you want." He raised his voice. "But I'm going around the back and coming in through the ocean side."

He walked away from her and a moment later heard her feet padding after him.

"Wait for me," she said.

"Good." He leaned close to her and whispered, "We'll go up this trellis to the second floor."

"I—" she started, but Remo put a hand over her mouth.

"Whisper," he said.

"I thought we were going around the back."

"You're not too smart, are you?" Remo said. "I said that for them inside."

"Why?"

He pointed over the front door. "They've got microphones and cameras all over the place. I don't want them to know what we're doing."

"Don't tell me you're afraid," Pamela said.

"Not for me," said Remo.

Pamela thought, then nodded. "All right. I'll be right behind you."

The second-floor window was open and Remo hoisted Pamela through before slipping inside himself. They were in a guest bedroom, whose walls, bedspread, furniture, rug, and drapes were all a bright red.

"This room looks like a freaking hemorrhage," Remo said.

"I kind of like it," Pamela said.

"Great place to bleed to death," Remo said. "If they get you, I'll bring you up here to die."

"Thank you. I'd really appreciate that," she said dryly.

The bedroom door opened onto a balcony which fronted all the rooms on the second floor and looked down into the large living and dining areas.

Remo gestured to Pamela for silence and brought her to the edge of the balcony. Below, they saw the three men hiding behind sofas and chairs, aiming guns at the sliding glass doors that led to an outside patio and the sandy beach beyond. The ocean looked very green today. It reminded Remo of the Caribbean.

"Should I shoot them?" she whispered softly in his ear.

"Why would you want to do that?"

"Get them before they get us. They've got us outgunned."

"Christ, you even think like James Bond," he said.

"Well, we can't just stand here until they all fall asleep," she hissed again.

He raised a hand to silence her. "Leave it to me," he said. He lightly vaulted over the railing and dropped the fifteen feet to the room below. He landed on the cushions of the sofa, rolled backward over its back, landed on his feet between two of the would-be gunmen, and snapped the machine guns from their hands.

The man behind the chair heard the sound and turned toward him, slowly raising his Magnum to firing height. But before he could do anything with it, Remo had taken it from his hand. Remo stood there among the three men holding all three guns. Three guns were awkward, he realized. He tried holding one machine gun in each hand and the revolver under his chin but that wasn't comfortable.

"Who are you? What do you want?" the man behind the chair said.

"Just hold your horses," Remo said. It was hard to talk holding a gun under your chin.

He put both machine guns under one arm and held the pistol in his other hand, but the machine guns began to slip. They might fall out, go off and hurt somebody that way, he thought.

"Are you all right?" Pamela yelled from the balcony.

"Fine, fine, fine, fine," Remo said. "Will you all just wait a minute?"

Finally he gave up and tossed all three weapons into a corner of the room. "Listen," he told the three men. "I put them over there but that doesn't mean you should think you can run over and get one or something because then I'll have to kill you."

Pamela came down the steps into the living room. She covered the three men with her small pistol and Remo noticed that she held it low and close to her hip, the way people did who were expert in the law-enforcement use of firearms, not out in front of her where anyone could slap it away.

"Don't anybody move," she snarled.

"They weren't planning to move, Mrs. Peel," Remo said sarcastically. "Now aim that thing away from me." He turned back to the three men. "Okay, what're your names?"

"Who wants to know?" said the man who had been hiding behind the chair.

Remo upended the brass coffee table behind the couch and twisted one of its legs into a corkscrew shape.

"Next question?" he said.

"Bondini," the man said. "Bernie Bondini."

Remo glanced at the other two men, who were still on the floor, cringing in front of Pamela, whose gun pointed unwaveringly at them.

"Hubble."

"Franko."

"Any of those sound like the voice that's been calling?" Remo asked Pamela.

"I can't tell from just their names," Pamela said. "They've got to say more."

"Who are you?" Bondini asked.

"Will you stop saying that?" Remo said. "All right. Now I want you to take turns. One at a time, repeat this: Four score and something ago, our forefathers brought up—"

"You're getting it wrong," Bondini said.

"Just say it any way you want," Remo said. "I never told you I was any good at history."

"Four score and seven years ago, our fathers brought forth upon—"

"That's good," Remo said. "You remember that from school?"

"Yes," said Bondini.

"I could never remember it," Remo said. "I kept mixing up fathers and forefathers. I was supposed to recite it on Memorial Day but I kept getting it wrong."

"That's a shame," Bondini said.

"Yeah. They got Romeo Rocco to do it instead. Boy, did he stink. He sounded like that guy who does the fast commercials. He wet his pants in the middle and he still finished the speech before any liquid reached the floor."

He turned back to Pamela.

"Him?" he asked. She shook her head no.

"Okay, you," Remo said, pointing to the bearded man on the floor. "What's your name?"

"Hubble."

"Okay. Recite the Gettysburg Address."

"I don't know the zip code for Gettysburg," Hubble said.

"Very funny," Remo said. "Now will you try for a broken neck?"

"Four score and seven years ago, our fathers something something," Hubble said.

"Him?" Remo asked Pamela.

"No," she said.

"That leaves you," Remo said to Franko. "Recite."

"Four score and seven years ago our fathers brought
forth upon this continent a new nation, conceived
in—"

"That's enough," Remo said.

"—liberty and dedicated to the proposition that all
men are created equal. Now we are engaged in a great
civil war, testing whether . . ." Stash Franko rose to
his feet. ". . . this nation or any nation, so conceived
and so dedicated—"

"I said enough," Remo said.

". . . can long endure. We are met on a great battlefield—"

Remo clapped his hand over Franko's mouth. "If
there's anything I hate, it's a show-off." He looked at
Pamela and she again shook her head no.

"I'm letting you go," Remo told Franko. "If you
promise to speak only when spoken to. You promise?"

Franko nodded and Remo released him.

"—of that war. We have come to dedicate a portion—"

Remo straightened out the brass table leg, snapped
it from the table, then wrapped it around Franko's
neck, tightly enough to frighten him, not so tight that
it would hurt him.

"I'll be quiet," Franko said meekly.

"What do you want?" Bondini said.

"Who's Buell? The owner?" Remo asked.

"We just met him once," Bondini said. "Abner Buell.
A twerpy-looking guy with plastic hair. I don't even
really know him."

Remo looked at the other two men, who shook their
heads.

"Why were you going to kill us then?" Remo asked.

"Because I didn't want to beat my mother with a stick," Bondini said.

"And I won't make it with no sheep," said Hubble.

"Or a corpse," said Franko.

It took Remo a while to sort it all out but with Pamela's help, he finally figured out that the three men were counting on getting some money from the owner of the place and they didn't even know who Remo was. He was glad about that because it meant that he would not have to kill them.

"How were you supposed to notify Buell that I was dead?" Remo asked.

"He didn't tell us."

Remo said to Pamela, "That means this place is wired or something. Probably sound and camera."

He turned back to the three men. "All right. You guys can go."

"That's it?" Bondini asked.

"You're not going to turn us in?" asked Hubble.

"Not me, pal. Go in peace."

Franko was silent, gazing out toward the ocean. Finally he said, "There was one thing."

"What was that?"

"The guy who owns this place. I heard him say he had a place just like it in Carmel and he was expecting company. Does that help?"

"Yes," Remo said. "Thanks."

"It's better than making it with a corpse," Franko said as he walked toward the door. He paused in the doorway.

"Another thing," he said.

"What?" said Remo.

". . . of this battlefield as a final resting place for those who here gave—" he said, and then ran as Remo started toward him.

*   *   *

In Carmel, north along the Pacific shoreline, Buell turned off the television monitor and said to Mr. Hamuta, "Get yourself ready. He should be here soon."

"I am always ready," Hamuta said.

"You'd better be."

Hamuta left and Marcia came into the room. Buell graced her with one of his infrequent and emotionless smiles. She was wearing a train engineer's outfit, but the legs of the jeans were cut off almost to her crotch and she had on no shirt and her breasts bobbled back and forth under the overalls' bib front.

"He escaped, this Remo?" she said.

"Yes."

"Who can he be?" she asked.

"Some government spy. I don't know," said Buell.

"Too bad he escaped," she said.

"No, it isn't. He was supposed to, remember? I just wanted him to be on his guard when he gets here. Make it a tougher game for Hamuta."

"Suppose Hamuta fails?" the woman asked.

"He never fails."

"But if he does?" the redhead persisted.

Buell rubbed a hand over his patent-leathered hair. "It doesn't matter," he said. "The whole world still goes up. Boom."

"I can't wait," Marcia said. "I can't wait."

Chapter Ten

"He flew the coop, Smitty," Remo said. "But I know who he is."

"Who?" asked Smith, whose computers had discovered the Malibu house but had not been able to identify its owner.

"Abner Buell."

"*The* Abner Buell?" asked Smith.

"An," said Remo.

"An?"

"He's *an* Abner Buell. That's all I know. I don't know if he's *the* Abner Buell. I don't even know who *the* Abner Buell is. *An.* But I think I know where he went. We're going there now."

"We?"

"The girl I'm with."

"Does she know who you are?" Smith asked.

"No. She thinks I work for the post office. No. The phone company."

"Get rid of her then," Smith said.

"She knows Buell's voice."

"And you know his name. I'm sure you'll be able to figure it out when you meet him. Get rid of her."

"Okay," Remo said.

"Where is Buell now?" Smith asked.

"I think he's got a place in Carmel. That's in California."

"Let me see if I can find it," Smith said. He fiddled with his computer. "Do you know how I found out the address in Malibu?"

"No," Remo said.

"Do you care?" Smith asked.

"Not even one whit," Remo said.

Smith snorted. "I've got an address in Carmel. It's probably his."

"I'll try it," Remo said and Smith gave him the address.

"By the way, Remo. Buell's got a very interesting background. Are you interested?"

"No."

"I beg your pardon," Smith said.

"That's okay," Remo said.

"What is okay?"

"Look. You asked me if I was interested in Buell's background. I said no. Does it have to get more complicated than that?"

"I guess not," Smith said slowly.

"Then we're done," Remo said.

"Remember. The man is capable of causing World War III. He's come very close in the last few days. Extreme measures are called for," Smith said.

"You mean, make pâté out of him."

"I mean make sure he can never do this again."

"Same thing," Remo said. "Good-bye."

*   *   *

Pamela Thrushwell was not pleased.

"I'm sorry," she said curtly, in her crispest British accent, "but I'm going."

"No, you're not. I'll handle this myself."

"No, thank you very much. I'm going, I said."

"And I said you're not," Remo said.

"Then I'll call the papers and tell them everything that's going on. Would you like that?"

"You wouldn't do that," Remo said.

"How are you going to stop me? Kill me?"

"It's a thought," Remo admitted.

"How will your superiors like that?" she asked.

"After the initial furor dies down, they'll raise the price of stamps. That's what they always do."

"You said you worked for the phone company, not the post office."

"I meant the price of a telephone call," Remo said.

"All right," she said. "You go. I don't need you. I can get a lift and go by myself."

Remo sighed. Why was everybody so intractable these days? Whatever happened to women who said yes and did what you wanted?"

"Okay. You can tag along. I guess that's the only way to keep you out of trouble."

"And you drive carefully," Pamela said.

"I will. I promise," Remo said. He also promised himself that when the appropriate time came, and he had Buell nailed, he would just leave Pamela on the side of the road somewhere and never see her again. As they left Malibu, going north along the coast highway, Pamela said, "Why'd you change your mind?"

"You've got a nice ass," Remo said.

"That's a dumb reason."

"Not if you're an ass man," Remo said.

"Who was that you called?" Pamela asked.

"My mother," Remo said. "She worries when I'm out of town too long. She worries about rain and snow and gloom of night keeping me from the swift completion of my appointed rounds."

"That's the post office again," she said.

"Don't nitpick," Remo said.

Mr. Hamuta was alone in the Carmel house, built overlooking the ocean on the town's fourteen-mile-long scenic coast drive. The entrance to the house was down a long winding pathway that began at the home's heavily locked front gates.

When Buell and Marcia had left, the redhead had asked, "Should we leave the front gate open?"

"No," Buell said.

"Why not?"

"Because the gate won't stop him whether it's locked or unlocked. But if we leave it unlocked, he might suspect a trap. Don't you agree, Mr. Hamuta?"

"Most wholeheartedly," Hamuta said. He was in an upstairs bedroom. The large windows had been opened and, sitting back from the glare of daylight, he was hidden from sight but commanded a total view of the walk and the gate and the roadway beyond.

"Suppose he comes from the ocean side?" Marcia asked.

"Mr. Hamuta has a television monitor," Buell said. "He can watch the ocean side." He pointed to the small television set which he had hooked up in the room, which showed a continuous panning shot of the Pacific.

"It is all quite adequate," Hamuta said. He was wearing a three-piece suit. His vest was tightly buttoned, his tie immaculately knotted and held in place by a collar pin on his expensive white-on-white shirt. "You choose not to remain for the entertainment?"

"Where we're going is hooked up to the house monitors here. We'll watch it on television."

"Very good. Will you tape it for me?" Hamuta said. "I would like to look at it when I return to Britain."

"You just love blood, don't you, Mr. Hamuta?" Buell said.

Hamuta did not answer. The truth was that he regarded the young American as too crass and too vulgar for words. Blood. What did he know about blood? Or about death? The young Yank designed games in which mechanical creatures died by the tens of thousands. What could he have experienced that would bear any resemblance to the feeling of exhilaration that came when a perfectly placed bullet brought down a human target so that other bullets, perfectly placed also, could carve him like a Christmas goose?

Had Buell ever held his index finger on a trigger and looked down the length of a perfect weapon and for the moment it took to apply the fractional ounce of pressure to the trigger, experienced the knowledge that one was not, at that moment, a mortal anymore but a god, infused with the power of life and death? What did this insignificant creature know about such things, he with his childish visions of fantasy games?

Mr. Hamuta thought these things but said nothing and watched silently as Buell and the woman—a strange one, that, and much brighter than she appeared to be—walked up the long curving walkway toward the road where a parked car waited.

Hamuta was glad to be alone, to savor the pleasure of the upcoming moments in silence, thinking to himself how he would place the bullets and where. The man was the important target so he would take the man first. He would put a shot in the knee. No, the hip. A hip shot caused more pain and would immobi-

lize the man. Then he would simply remove the woman
with one shot and then go back to the man and carve
him up with bullets. It was so much more fun that
way. Buell was wrong. Hamuta was not interested in
death for death's sake. He was interested in killing for
killing's sake. The act of the kill was pure and worthy.

When the afternoon shadows began to lengthen,
Hamuta took a telescope from a velvet-lined box and
carefully mounted it atop his rifle. Using a magnifying glass, he lined up a series of marks atop the scope
with matching marks on the rifle frame itself, locking
the telescope into the correct firing focus. The scope
was a light-gathering instrument of a highly complicated personal design but it was able to render objects
seen in dim light as highly illuminated, as if they
were being viewed at high noon under a bright sun.

Then, telescope in place, again he sat, the rifle
cradled in his arms like an infant, and waited.

The man first. It would definitely be the man first.

Three thousand miles away, Harold W. Smith looked
at the printed report that his computers had spewed
out on Abner Buell.

Brilliant. Unquestionably brilliant.

But unstable. Unquestionably unstable.

The computer issued a list of properties held by
Buell and companies in which he was an investor.
The dry tedium that makes up a person's life, Smith
thought.

There was one small item buried at the end of the
report. It said that a British computer had malfunctioned and almost resulted in Great Britain announc-
ing it was leaving NATO and signing a friendship
pact with Russia. Access to the British computers
was by satellite signal from the United States, the

computer report stated. Probability of Buell's involvement: sixty-three percent.

A wacko, Smith thought. A wacko tired of playing game-games and now ready to start World War III, the biggest game of all.

He hoped Remo would be in time to stop him.

Remo had tried to dump her by the side of the road when he stopped at a gas station and said he had to use the bathroom. As he expected, she said she did too. He went into the men's room, then darted right back out, jumped in the car and drove away. But something didn't feel right and he figured out what it was just before Pamela stuck her head up from the back seat, where she had been hiding on the floor, and said, "If you try that again, Yank, I'll plug you."

So now they were standing in front of the locked gate of Buell's Carmel mansion and Remo snapped open the lock and pushed the gate open. It swung soundlessly, well-oiled, no squeak.

"You shouldn't come in," he said.

"Why not?"

"It might be dangerous."

"This is California. You think it's not dangerous for me to sit in a car by the side of the road? I'm coming in," she said.

"All right. But you be careful."

"I have my gun."

"That's what I want you to be careful of. I don't want you to go shooting me by accident."

"If I shoot you, it won't be by accident," Pamela Thrushwell sniffed, then followed him down the short flight of steps that led to the twisting flagstone path.

*　　*　　*

It was perfect.

The two were off the steps now, onto the path, and Hamuta raised the rifle to his shoulder. The telescope intensified the dim light and brightened the images of the two people walking toward the house.

Perfect.

First the man. A bullet in the hip to drop and immobilize him. Then the woman. Then return to the man.

Perfect.

"Don't look now," Remo said, "but there's somebody in that upstairs window."

Pamela started to look up and Remo pulled her toward him by the wrist. "I said, don't look up."

"I didn't see anybody up there," she said.

"You're not supposed to. Just walk naturally."

He let go of her wrist. They walked a few more steps. Remo stopped and grabbed her arm again.

"What . . . ?"

"Shh," he said. He felt the pressure waves increasing on his body. He did not know what he sensed or how he sensed it, but there was a faint pressure, circling in on him, invisibly touching him, a caress of danger.

"There's a weapon on us," he said softly.

"How do you know?"

"I know is all. Upstairs window. Wait. Wait. *Now!*"

He pushed her aside as a shot cracked. She hit the soft grassy earth and rolled behind a large stone that decorated the home's flower-bedecked front garden.

Remo had spun into a double spiral. The shot had been meant for his right hip. He knew it without knowing it and he went heavily down onto the stone path.

"Remo," Pamela called. She started for her feet.

He lay heavily on the stone path. "Just shut up and stay there," he hissed. "No matter what happens."

Hamuta smiled. The white man lay on the ground, still, his right hip jutting out from his body at a harsh, unreal angle. Hamuta knew he had hit the ball joint just the way he wanted to.

But the damned woman. She had slipped behind the rock, out of his sight.

He waited a moment, rifle still raised to his shoulder, then shook his head. He did not like changes in his program but he was going to have to make one. He would dispose of the man first and then take care of the woman.

He looked again at Remo.

Perhaps this time, the left hip.

Remo felt the second shot before he heard the sound.

In the fraction of a fraction of a second before the bullet reached him, he sensed its direction, its velocity, its intended target and, at the last moment, jerked his body off the ground. The bullet hit the flagstone below his left hip and he could feel shards of stone spray upward against his side. He settled back, twitched and groaned. Behind him, he could hear the rebounding slug whistling off across the road.

Pamela groaned. "Oh, no."

Remo twitched.

For a moment, Hamuta thought about removing the man's earlobes but he decided against it. There was no fun in it, a simple bullet in the heart would be best and fastest. Then go downstairs, find the woman and dispose of her too. She might prove to be more fun.

He lined up the sight with Remo's chest and squeezed the trigger.

Pamela Thrushwell was looking toward the house when she saw the flash from a gun's muzzle just inside the second-floor window. Then she heard the crack. She spun to the left, just in time to see Remo's body crumple, as if folding itself around something. It jerked back, three feet, rolled once and then lay facedown, arms sprawled out.

Hamuta did not like physical movement but not even his favorite weapon could fire through the rock behind which the young woman was hiding. He came out of the house and glanced up the slight incline to where Remo's body lay still. He was disappointed; he had wanted to have more sport with the man. Three shots, two hips and a heart, were not even enough to whet his appetite. It had been a very unspectacular, unsatisfying kill, and he would be glad to leave this barbarian country and return to a civilized land where even dying had rules and gentlemen observed them.

He walked up the path, rifle held loosely at his right side. The woman might be armed, he thought randomly. Well, it didn't matter. Women were just simply hopeless with firearms. She would be no threat; it would be no contest.

Before he reached the young white man's body, he stepped off the path and headed on a straight line for the large stone. He moved silently over the well-trimmed grass and when he reached the rock, he stopped and listened. Clearly, he heard her breathing and he smiled slightly to himself.

He bent over and picked up a small stone, made moist by the Pacific air. He moved silently to the right side of the stone, nearest the walkway, then tossed the pebble over the stone's other end.

It hit with a small sound, rippling through a flowering azalea bush. Without waiting, Hamuta moved around the right side of the rock.

He was confronted by Pamela Thrushwell's back. She stood in firing position, looking away from him, toward where the sound had come from, and before she could move, Hamuta had stepped toward her and knocked the pistol from her hand.

She wheeled to see the elegantly dressed little man, holding a rifle at his side, and smiling at her.

"Who the sod are you?" she demanded.

Hamuta smiled at her coarse British accent. The woman might be a battler and that was good. It might redeem what had so far been a very dull day.

"I am going to give you a chance to escape," Hamuta said. "You may run."

"So you can shoot me in the back?"

"I will not shoot until you are least twenty-five yards away," he said. "A twenty-five-yard head start." He smiled. "Because we are both British."

"No."

"Then I will shoot you here," Hamuta said.

Pamela's eyes strayed toward the ground where her pistol had fallen.

"You will not be able to reach it before I fire," he said. He had backed up so he was five feet away from the woman, far enough so that no sudden lunge of hers could reach the rifle before his bullet reached her brain.

A sudden jolt of fear surged in Pamela. For a moment, she seemed undecided whether to run or to take a chance on diving for the gun, hoping that a lucky shot would get the man before he got her. He seemed able to read her mind. He said, "Run and you have a chance. A small chance but a chance. Move for that pistol and you have none. Now run."

And then there was another voice that rang out over the lawn. It came from behind Hamuta.

"Not so fast, butterball."

Hamuta wheeled. Remo stood on the walkway, fifteen feet away, looking at him. The young American's eyes were dark and cold and in the lengthening evening, shadows carved his face into harsh angular planes.

Hamuta's jaw dropped open in shock.

"How are you there?" he asked, almost to himself as much as Remo.

"I'm a fast healer. I always was. Pamela, is that the voice?"

She was unable to answer. Surprise and shock had frozen her tongue.

"I said is that the voice?" Remo repeated.

"No," she finally coughed.

"I didn't think so. Okay. Where's Buell?" Remo asked the man in the three-piece suit.

Hamuta had recovered. Somehow he must have missed. But not at this distance. He still would have some fun with the thin American.

"I'm talking to you, suethead," Remo said.

He stepped forward and Hamuta, smiling, raised the rifle slowly to his shoulder. He had forgotten Pamela behind him and she moved quietly toward her pistol. She heard Hamuta say, "Your right shoulder, first." She lunged for the pistol. Perhaps she could get the Englishman before he got Remo. But then she heard the rifle's whip-snap crack.

She looked up. Remo still stood there, smiling, his body twisted slightly so that his left shoulder was forward, toward Hamuta.

"What? What? What?" Hamuta was sputtering. He could not believe he had missed. Neither could Pamela.

Angrily this time, Hamuta squeezed the trigger again, aiming at Remo's midsection only a few feet away from him. As Pamela watched, Remo's body seemed to twist, then unravel. It was a rolling motion that had no discernible rhythm to it, no predictability, and Hamuta, with Remo now only eight feet away, fired another shot but Remo kept moving forward. The bullet must have missed. But Pamela knew that the Englishman could not miss forever at this distance so she aimed at his head, holding both hands on the butt of the pistol.

As she squeezed the trigger, she heard Remo call out: "No."

But it was too late. The pistol barked and the back of Hamuta's head exploded and he dropped face-forward onto the grass. Blood ran down the sides of his head. The rifle lay under his body. Remo looked over at Pamela.

"What the hell did you go and do that for?" he said.

"He was going to kill you."

"If he was able to kill me, he would have done it a half a dozen shots ago," Remo grumbled. "Now he's dead and I don't know who he is or where Buell is or anything. And it's all your fault."

"Stop sniveling," she said.

"I knew it was a mistake to let you come along."

"I never got less thanks for trying to save someone's life," Pamela said.

"Save it for the Red Cross," Remo said. "I don't need it."

"You really are an ungrateful wretch," Pamela said. "I thought you were dead. If you weren't hurt, why'd you wait so long?"

"Because, bigmouth, I had to see if there were others. Because if I went after him, one of his partners, if he had any, might have gotten you. Because I was thinking about keeping you alive, even if only God knows why. Because if it's not one irritation, it's another."

Pamela thought for a moment and was about to say thank you, but the scowl on Remo's face soured her and she said, "You can stay here and complain if you want, but I'm going inside the house."

"Buell's not there," Remo said.

"How do you know?"

"Because the house is empty."

"How do you know that?" she asked.

"I just know."

"I'll look for myself," Pamela said.

The house was empty. Remo followed her inside and in the upstairs bedroom saw the television monitor which patrolled the ocean-side back of the house.

"I'll bet that bastard is monitoring what goes on here," Remo said.

"Maybe."

"Sure. He's *the* Abner Buell. I bet he's a big TV wizard or something. He's been watching. He knows that Tubby the Tuba out there is dead. He was probably watching the place at Malibu too. That's how he knew we were coming here."

"Maybe," she said.

"Look." Remo pointed toward the ceiling. "There. And there. Those are all television cameras." He walked out into the hallway. "Sure," he called back. "He's got them all over. Right now, he's someplace watching us."

Pamela's hand moved instinctively to her throat to adjust the collar of her blouse.

Remo walked toward one of the cameras, looked at

it, and said aloud, "Buell, if you're listening. This is the last time you're going to mess around with the telephone company. I'm coming for you. You understand? I'm coming for you."

As he ripped the camera from the ceiling, he said, again, "I'm coming for you. If you're watching."

Chapter Eleven

". . . if you're watching."

Abner Buell was watching and the last thing he saw was Remo's hand extend upward toward the hidden camera and then the screen went black.

It had all been a game up till now, but suddenly, for an instant, he felt the hair raise along his arms and on the back of his neck. For he had looked into the televised image of Remo's dark eyes and felt as if he were looking into the face of hell.

Another television screen was next to him and as soon as the first screen went blank, bells began to ring on the second, small multicolored cartoon figures marched across the board, and then were replaced by a neat precise drawing of a man in a three-piece suit lying dead. Mr. Hamuta.

The machine spelled out a message to Buell.

"Target Remo now worth five hundred thousand points. Last defender gone. Play options: 1) surrender and save life; 2) fight on alone. Chances of success: 21 percent."

"Who the hell asked you?" Buell snapped, and switched off the game screen.

Behind him, Marcia asked: "It is not going good, is it, Abner?"

He wheeled around. Marcia was wearing a French maid's costume, her breasts high and saucy in a push-up bra. Her legs were encased in black mesh stockings that ended high up her white thighs with a black garter belt. A small black apron with a white lace fringe completed the costume.

Buell said, "Not going good? I haven't even started. What the hell does the computer know?" He looked at her costume again, seeming to notice it for the first time.

"I like the harem pants better. Wear them. With nothing on underneath. And the little gauze vest. I like that. Don't button it."

"As you wish, Abner," she said, but she did not leave immediately. "What do you plan to do now?"

"Why are you asking so many questions today? You going for Barbara Walters' job? Why don't you go back to modeling?"

"I am just interested in you," she said evenly. "You are the most remarkable man I have ever met and I want to know how your mind works."

As he turned back to the computer, he said, "Brilliantly. Brilliantly."

He turned on the machine and hunched his shoulders as he leaned over the keyboard. Marcia watched him for a few long seconds, but when it was clear he was not going to speak again, she left to change her costume.

Buell did not hear her leave. He was working over the computer, creating a program and inserting data as rapidly as most people could type.

His first thought was to find out how this Remo, whoever he was, had traced him accurately in Malibu and in Carmel. Had Buell himself made it too easy?

But neither house was listed under his name. None of his neighbors in Carmel—and they were all far distant on both sides of his home—even knew him and as far as he knew had never even seen him. If Remo had come to Carmel and asked for Abner Buell's home, all he would have gotten was a blank stare.

How had he found it so easily?

He sat at the machine, asking the computer different questions, getting answers that did not satisfy him. He waited for the computer to solve the puzzle but it did not. And then, in one of those leaps of intuition that he felt would always separate man's mind from the machine mind, he asked the machine: "What about utility bills?"

The computer did not understand. Its screen lit up with a line of question marks.

"What home is biggest private user of electricity in Malibu?" he asked.

The computer responded: "Wait. Tapping into utility-company computer records."

Buell drummed his fingers on the side of the console while he waited. In less than a minute, the computer responded. It gave Buell's own Malibu address.

Buell smiled. Maybe, he thought. Maybe. He typed onto the monitor: "What home is largest private user of electricity in Carmel?"

The machine again begged for time, and then listed the address of Buell's Carmel home.

He snapped his fingers and whooped. He had found it. Remo had found his addresses by checking the electrical usage in both communities. It was a fair assumption that Buell, with his computers and cameras and cybernetic equipment and design studios, would have been high on that list.

It was a trail that this Remo, whoever he was, had been able to follow.

But trails led in both directions.

Buell knew that Remo was no free-lance. He was working for someone, some agency which was disturbed at Buell's activities over the last several months.

The trail that led from that agency to Buell could also lead back, if Buell could only follow it, if he could only read the signs. But how to do it?

He sat silently at the console for a long time, thinking. The computer, never bored, never impatient, waited for his instructions.

Finally Buell moved. He directed the computer to go back into the utility company and find out who, besides himself, had dug into its computers to get the addresses of large electricity users.

The computer gave a listing of all such queries for the Malibu area. A few minutes later, it gave the similar listing for Carmel.

Buell typed into the computer: "List all duplicates." The computer instantly responded that only one name had appeared on both lists. It was a small computer laboratory in Colorado.

Buell instructed the computer to slip into the Colorado lab's equipment and find out if the queries had been generated from there or had been merely passed through there.

While he waited for a response, Marcia reentered the room but he did not see her. The computer's ready light flashed and gave him the name of a printing supply house in Chicago as the originator of the queries. Buell smiled. He knew he was on the right track now. What reason could a printing-supply house

in the Midwest have to want to know the electrical
bills at two California coastal towns? None at all. The
Chicago company was a cover.

Again he instructed the machine to tap into the
Chicago computers and follow the query back.

It took two hours. The trail led from the Chicago
company to an auto-parts firm in Secaucus, New Jersey.
Then back to an Oriental food company in Seneca
Falls, New York, and then to a restaurant on West
Twenty-sixth Street in New York.

From there, the computers traced the query to a
distributor of used tractor parts in Rye, New York.

And there it stopped.

"Continue trace," Buell ordered the computer.

"No further lead," the computer flashed back.
"Query on electrical usage originated in Rye, New
York, computer."

Buell again stared at the monitor. Unseen and forgotten by him was Marcia, who sat in a corner of the
room quietly watching. She was wearing her houri
outfit and while she was proud of her body, she knew
it would bring no sign of interest from him. Not now.
Not while he was working. And above all, she wanted
him to keep working.

She heard Buell giggle and somehow knew it was a
dirty trick he had planned.

"Find greatest privacy electricity consumption in
Rye, New York," he said.

The computer worked silently for only fifteen seconds before reporting the name and address of a Dr.
Harold W. Smith.

"Information on Smith," Buell demanded.

Short minutes later, the computer reported: "Director
of Folcroft Sanitarium, Rye, New York."

"Nature of Folcroft Sanitarium?" Buell typed.

"Private nursing home for elderly mental patients," the computer responded.

"Is monthly utility bill of Folcroft Sanitarium consistent with utility bills of similar private nursing homes?" Buell asked.

It took the machine fifteen minutes to issue a reply. Finally, it printed out: "No. Electrical usage excessive."

"Consistent with heavy computer operation?" Buell asked.

"Yes," the machine responded almost instantly.

Buell turned off the computer, satisfied that he had tracked down the truth. It took a massive computer operation to track down his two homes at Malibu and Carmel, and that computer operation was centered in Rye, New York. It stood to reason that the man in charge of it would have heavy-duty terminals in his home: thus, the excessive use of electricity at the home of Dr. Harold W. Smith.

And the Folcroft Sanitarium that Smith headed. That too used too much electricity for just a simple nursing home. Again, a computer operation.

This Remo had been sent by this Smith. And this Smith whoever he was, ran something important in the United States. Something important and dangerous to Abner Buell.

It was late at night and Harold Smith was preparing to leave his darkened office at Folcroft. His secretary had gone hours before and he knew that dinner would be waiting for him when he arrived home, some kind of meat smothered in some kind of red catsuppy goo.

He had reached the door of his office when one of his private telephone lines rang. Remo. It must be

Remo, he thought, and he strode quickly across the antistatic carpet to the telephone.

But the voice that answered his "hello" was not Remo's.

"Dr. Smith?" the voice said.

"Yes."

"This is Abner Buell. I think you've been looking for me?"

Chapter Twelve

Smith looked toward the icy waters of Long Island Sound, two hundred yards away, lapping at the rocky shoreline where the manicured lawns of Folcroft fell away before finally surrendering to the salt-laced air.

The remnants of a rickety old dock stuck out into the water, bent at strange angles like an arthritic finger. God, so long ago. It was to that very dock that Smith and another ex-CIA man, now long dead, had tied up their small boat when they came to Folcroft to set up CURE. So many years ago.

And so many disappointments.

They had been filled with high hopes for the secret organization's success and it had failed. It had won some little fights, some small skirmishes, but the big criminals, the overlords and chieftains, all kept getting away with crime because the justice system was weighted in favor of the rich and powerful. A successful prosecution was a chain of many links and it was always possible to corrupt and weaken one of those links and break the chain.

Smith had been prepared to write CURE off, call it

a failure, and go back to New Hampshire and life as a college professor. But then he and CURE were given permission to recruit an enforcement arm—one man— to mete out the punishment that the legal system couldn't and wouldn't mete out.

Remo Williams had been the man. Smith had framed the orphan policeman for a killing he didn't commit, had seen him sentenced to die in an electric chair that didn't work, and had brought him to Folcroft for training. Ten years ago. And for that decade, it had often been only Remo, trained by Chiun and supported by Smith, to stand up for America against all its enemies.

And it had all started with that small power boat tying up to that rickety old dock.

So many years ago.

So many deaths ago.

Conrad MacCleary, the other CIA agent, was dead many years now, and Smith ruefully reflected that he too was dead in a way. Certainly the Smith who had come to this place to start CURE, filled with optimism and high hopes, no longer existed. That Smith had been replaced by a man who ate tension as his daily diet, who hoped finally not to wipe out crime and criminals, but merely to try to stay even with them. The young Harold Smith was dead, as dead as if he lay in a grave.

And now, it was Remo's turn.

Remo or America. That was the price Abner Buell had set, and Smith knew that it was a price he would pay.

At first, Smith had thought he was talking to a madman, because Buell kept talking about Remo's point value continuing to go up as he got tougher and tougher to destroy.

He *was* mad, but he was also crafty and intelligent and dangerous. He had told Smith about the aborted U.S. missile firing which was a whistle away from beginning World War III and he told Smith about a similar Russian event, about which Smith was only now starting to get information. Buell stated proudly that he was behind both moves. He had too much solid information for Smith to disbelieve him and Smith's stomach sank when Buell said he could do it all again if he chose.

And he would so choose. Unless Remo was removed from the board.

"Think about it, Dr. Smith," Buell had said. "You get rid of that Remo. Or I'll start a nuclear war."

"Why would you do that?" Smith asked placantly. "You'd probably die too in an all-out nuclear war."

Buell had cackled, a madman's laugh. "Maybe and maybe not. But it'd be my war. I'd be the winner because I started it and that was what I set out to do. Five million extra points for starting a nuclear war. It's this Remo or that. Make up your mind."

"I have to think about it," Smith said, stalling for time as his Folcroft computers raced through switching procedures to try to trace the phone call.

"I'll call you tomorrow then," Buell said. "Oh, by the way. Your computers won't be able to trace this call."

"Why not?" Smith asked.

"They haven't had time yet. All they'll know is I'm someplace west of the Mississippi, and that's right. Good-bye."

That had been an hour ago and still Smith sat looking through the smoky windows at the sound. The United States or Remo. Maybe the world or Remo.

When it was that simple, was there any question

what his response would be? Sighing, he picked up
the telephone to call Chiun.

Marcia tried to make him eat dinner, but Buell
curtly told her he was too busy.

World War III—five million points.

Remo—a half-million points.

Pamela Thrushwell—fifty thousand points by now.

And now this Dr. Smith? How many points to give
him?

He turned on the television monitor's game board
and watched the point totals appear on the screen.
Smith was a bureaucrat probably, and probably dumb.
Arbitrarily, he decided to give Harold W. Smith a
mere ten thousand points.

Until further calculation.

In the middle of the hotel-room floor, surrounded
by piles of bond paper, Chiun sat.

Smith waited, silent, until Chiun acknowledged his
presence but the old Oriental was preoccupied. As
Smith watched, Chiun was busy crossing out type-
written lines and writing in other lines, using a quill
pen and an old-fashioned inkwell which he had on the
floor before him. His tongue stuck slightly out of one
corner of his mouth, showing his concentration. His
hands flew so rapidly over the paper that to Smith
they seemed almost a blur in the dimly lit room.
Finally, Chiun sighed and placed the quill pen down,
next to the inkwell. The motion was casual but grace-
ful and when he was done, inkwell and pen looked as
if they had been sculpted from one piece of black
stone.

Without looking up, Chiun said, "Greetings, O
Emperor. Your servant apologizes for his ill manners.

Had I but known you were here, all else would have been relegated to unimportance. How may I serve you?"

Smith, who knew Chiun's excuse was nonsense since the Oriental would have recognized him a corridor away by the sound of his feet scuffing on a thick carpet, looked at the stacks of paper on the floor.

"Are you writing something?" he asked.

"A poor thing but an honest effort. One in which you may well take pride, Emperor."

"This isn't one of those petitions you got up to Stop Amateur Assassins, is it?" Smith asked warily.

Chiun shook his head. "No. I have decided that the time is not yet right for a national movement dedicated to obliterating inferior work. Someday but not now." He waved a long-nailed hand over the papers. "This is a novel. I am writing a novel."

"Why?"

"Why? Because the world needs beauty. And it is a good way for a man to spend his days, telling what he has learned so he can lighten the burden of those who are yet to come."

"This isn't about you, is it? About us?"

Chiun chuckled and shook his head. "No, Emperor. I understand full well your lust for secrecy. This has nothing to do with any of us."

"What's it about then?" Smith asked.

"It is about a noble old Oriental assassin, the last of his line, and the white ingrate he tries to teach and the secret agency that employs them. A mere trifle."

Suddenly, Smith remembered the bizarre call he had gotten earlier from some publisher who had thought that Folcroft was a training area for assassins. "I thought you said it wasn't about us," Smith said.

"And it is not," Chiun said innocently.

"But a noble old Oriental assassin. His white student. A secret agency. Master of Sinanju, that is us," Smith said.

"No, no. Not even superficial similarities," Chiun said. "For instance, this Oriental assassin about whom I write is honored by the country which he has adopted and for which he works. Totally unlike my situation. And the white trainee, well, in my novel, he is not always ungrateful. And he is capable of learning something. Clearly that has nothing to do with Remo."

"The secret agency though," said Smith.

"Never once do I mention the Constitution and how we all work outside the Constitution so that everybody else can live inside it. How we break it so we can fix it." He gave Smith a sly grin. "Although I must confess that once I thought I might use that in my novel, but I realized no one would believe it. It is just too ridiculous to be believable."

"It still sounds a great deal like us," Smith said. "At least on a superficial level."

"You need not worry yourself about that, Emperor. The publisher has recommended certain changes which will dispel your fears. That is what I occupy myself with while Remo is away."

"What kind of changes?" Smith asked.

"Just a few. Everybody loves my manuscript. I just have to make a few changes for Bipsey Boopenberg in Binding and Dudley Sturdley in Accounting."

"What kind of changes?" Smith persisted.

"They assure me if I make these changes that I will become a big star and my book a best-seller. *The Needle's Eye* by Chiun. I have to change the Oriental assassin into a Nazi spy. The white trainee has to go. In place of the secret organization in America, I have to have Nazi spies in England. And set it in World

War II. And I have to have a woman who will save the world from destruction at the hands of that lunatic with the funny mustache. This is all they wanted changed. And then I will be rich."

"You are already rich, Master, in the things that count."

"And you are always kind, Emperor. But there is an old saying in Sinanju. Kindness can warm a soul but it cannot fill an empty belly."

Smith decided to drop the subject of Chiun's novel because he felt a con job coming on to raise Chiun's fees for training Remo. And besides, Chiun was always writing and never publishing, and there was no reason to think this book's fate would be any different.

And maybe none of it would matter anyway. Why worry about it today when it was possible that tomorrow, or just a few tomorrows away, none of them might be alive to worry about anything.

"I understand," Smith said simply. "Master, I come to speak to you about a matter of great importance."

"As important as my novel?" Chiun asked.

"Yes."

"Name your request, sire. It will be done," Chiun said.

"I'm glad you feel that way, Chiun. May I sit down?"

Chiun waved a hand airily toward the sofa. "Please. Be comfortable." He liked the gesture with his hand and repeated it. It would be the gesture he used when he was being interviewed by *Time* magazine for a cover story. Chiun, Great New Author. He would wave the reporter to a seat with just that gesture, elegant and imperious, but also inviting. He would serve tea to reporters. And read them Ung poetry to show them that his was the soul of a true artist. And he would keep Remo away from them because Remo was impos-

sible, incapable of even the simplest civility, and he
would certainly alienate the press. Or, at the very
least, he would wind up insinuating himself into the
story. Chiun had had enough of people thinking that
Remo was important when anyone with any sense
should know that Chiun was the important one.

Quietly, to himself, he wondered what Smith was
upset about now. His face was so long, his chin seemed
to be searching for his shoes. What was it about white
men, Americans particularly, that they always thought
everything was the end of the world? When the world
had gone on and would go on for ages beyond counting?
He told himself to humor Smith, as usual, and get rid
of him as soon as he could so he could get back to his
rewriting.

"What weighs so heavily on your spirit?" Chiun
asked.

"You remember when you first came to provide
services to us?" Smith asked.

"Indeed I do," Chiun said. "You have never missed
a payment, small though they may be."

"Your primary mission was to train Remo as our
enforcement arm."

"Assassin. I was to make him your assassin," Chiun
corrected.

"Yes," Smith said.

"You should not give a wonderful thing an awful
name. Enforcement arm is a terrible name," Chiun
said. He realized he was being very helpful to Smith,
much more so than the man deserved. When he tried
to advertise in the future for someone to replace Remo,
what kind of people would he be likely to get if he
advertised for "an enforcement arm"? But advertis-
ing for an assassin would bring the best minds, the
highest and most noble thinkers of the world to Smith's

court. So Chiun felt good about offering Smith this advice without any charge. Occasionally, it was good policy to do a favor for your emperor, just to remind him how much he truly relied on your wisdom and judgment.

"You have lived up to your end of the contract nobly," Smith said. "Your training of Remo has exceeded even what we hoped for from you."

"He is white. I have done the best I could, to overcome that handicap," Chiun said graciously.

"There was another part to the contract," Smith said in a low flat voice.

"Yes?"

"It was your promise that should the day ever come when Remo could not be used anymore by us, that you would ... you would remove him for us."

Chiun sat silently. Smith saw consternation on the old man's face.

Finally, Chiun said, "Go on."

"The time has come. Remo must be removed."

"What is your reason for this, Emperor?" Chiun asked slowly.

"It is complicated," Smith said. "But if Remo is allowed to live, the world may face a nuclear war."

"Oh, that," said Chiun, dismissing it with the raising of his eyebrows.

"Hundreds of millions will die," Smith intoned solemnly.

"Don't worry, Emperor. Remo and I will let nothing happen to you."

"Chiun, it's not me. It's the whole world. The whole world may explode. Remo must die."

"And I? I am supposed to kill him?" Chiun asked.

"Yes. It is your obligation under your contract."

"And this is so that we can save the lives of some millions of people?" Chiun said.

"Yes."

"Do you know anything about these millions of people?" Chiun asked.

"I—"

"No, you do not," Chiun said. "Well, I will tell you about them. Many of them are old and ready to die anyway. Most of them are ugly. Especially if they are white. Even more of them are stupid. Why sacrifice Remo for all these people we do not know? He is not much, but he is something. All those others, they are nothing."

"Chiun, I know how you feel, but—"

"You know nothing of how I feel," Chiun said. "I took Remo from nothing and now I have made of him something. In only ten more years of training, we could both be very proud of him. And now you are saying, Chiun, all the time you have spent on him is wasted and to be thrown away because somebody is going to blow up a lot of fat people. I understand the ways of emperors but this is rudeness beyond measure."

"We are talking about the end of the world," Smith huffed.

"It seems as if we are always talking about the end of the world," Chiun said. "Who is this person who threatens this? Is it one person? Remo and I will go to dispatch this person. He will never be seen again. He will have no descendants and those that now live will die. Friends too shall perish. All in the greater glory of the Emperor Smith and the Constitution."

"Master of Sinanju, I call upon you to honor your contract."

There was a long silence, broken only by Smith's

breathing. Finally, Chiun asked, "There is no other way?"

"If there were, I would take it," Smith said. "But there is none. I know that contracts are sacred to Masters of Sinanju and those were the terms of our contract. Upon request from me, you would remove Remo. I now make that request."

"You will leave me," Chiun said in a cold low voice that seemed to chill the skin on Smith's face.

At the doorway, the CURE director paused.

"What is your decision?"

"What you think important is my mission," Chiun said. "Contracts are made to be honored. It has been the way of my people for scores of centuries."

"You will do your duty," Smith said.

Chiun nodded once, slowly, then let his head sink to his chest. Smith left, quietly closing the door behind him.

And Chiun thought: White fool. Do you think that Remo is some piece of machinery to be discarded upon a whim?

He had trained Remo to be an assassin but Remo had become more than that. His body and his mind had accepted the trainings of Sinanju more thoroughly than anyone since Chiun. Remo now was a Master of Sinanju himself, and one day, upon Chiun's death, Remo would be reigning Master.

And by attaining that rank, Remo would fulfill a prophecy that had existed for ages in the House of Sinanju. That someday there would be as Master a white man who was dead but had come back to life and he would be the greatest Master of all, and of him it would be said that he was the avatar of the great god Shiva. Shiva the Destroyer. Remo.

And now Smith wanted him to throw all that away

because some fools planned to blow up some other
fools.

But yet, the contract was sacred. It was the corner-
stone upon which the House of Sinanju had been
built. Its word—once given by the Master in contract—
was inviolate. No Master had ever failed to carry out
the terms of a contract and Chiun, through thousands
of years of tradition, could not allow himself to be the
first.

He sat on the floor and slowly touched his fingertips to the temples of his bowed head.

The room grew dark with night and yet he did not
move, but the air in the room vibrated with the long
keening sounds of anguish that came from his lips.

Chapter Thirteen

"Why are we getting a motel room?" Pamela asked.

"Because I have to wait for a telephone call," Remo said. "You don't want to stay with me? Catch the next flight back and join the rest of the Lilliputians."

"Lilliputians?"

"From Liverpool. That's what people in Liverpool are called. Lilliputians," Remo patiently explained.

"No, they're not."

"Are too. I read it. The Beatles were Lilliputians."

"That's Liverpudlians," Pamela Thrushwell said.

"Is not."

"Is too," she said.

"I'm not going to stay here and try to educate you in speaking English correctly," Remo said. "Go home. Who needs you?"

That more than anything else convinced her to stay even though she looked with undisguised disgust at the dismal room, just like so many others in which Remo had spent so many nights. The furniture might have been called Utilitarian if it had not had a greater claim on being called Ugly. The walls, once white, were yellowed with the exhalations of countless smokers. The carpeting was indoor-outdoor rug, but looked as if it had not only been used outdoors but on the roadbed of the Lincoln Tunnel for the last twenty years. Threads showed through, masked only by dirt and embedded grime.

The toilet bowl had a dark ring around it at water level, the hot-water faucet in the sink didn't work, and the room's only luxury, an electric coffeepot in the bathroom, didn't work either. The place reeked with a faint smell of ammonia, as if from a cleaning solution, but the room resolutely refused to give up any clue as to where cleaning solution had ever been used in it.

"What are you here for anyway? What phone call are you waiting for?"

"I'm waiting to find out where Buell is," Remo said.

"I'd be better off trying to find him myself," Pamela said.

"Why don't you try?" Remo said hopefully.

"Because you're so hopeless that without me, you're liable to get hurt and then I'd feel guilty for causing it. For not staying around to take care of you."

"I promise not to come back and haunt your dreams," Remo said.

"You're pretty tenacious for somebody who's just supposed to be tracking down an obscene phone caller," she said.

"You too for somebody with just a tweaked titty," Remo said.

"That's gross. I'm staying."

"Do what you want," Remo said. He thought he'd rather have her tagging along for a while than argue with her. But he still didn't know why she wanted to stay.

Abner Buell did.

Outside the small central California town of Hernandez is a strange elevation of volcanic rock, rising fifty feet above the surrounding scrub grass. Abner Buell had bought the property and fifty surrounding acres three years earlier, and when he had seen the small mountain, he had hollowed it out and built inside it—separated from the outside world by fifteen-foot-thick walls of rock—a private apartment and laboratory.

He sat there now facing another of the computer consoles which he had in every home and apartment he occupied anywhere in the world.

It would be hours before he was to call Dr. Smith again, and he whiled away the time by reconfirming that he was able to tap into the Russian military-command computers.

Using satellite transmissions, he tapped into the Soviet system and amused himself by finding out actual troop strength in Afghanistan. He called up the number of spies in the Russian mission to the United Nations. The listing of names went on so long that Buell gave his computer simpler instructions:

"How many members of the Russian UN mission are *not* spies?"

The computer listed three names—the chief ambassador, a chauffeur second-grade, and a pastry chef named Pierre.

Pamela Thrushwell came into his mind and on a whim, he tapped the Russian KGB computer network and asked how many spies the Soviet Union had in-

side Great Britain. "Five-minute reading limit on lists,"
he wrote.

The computer responded: "List too lengthy. Russian nationals who are spies? Or British who work as
spies for USSR?"

He thought for a moment and asked: "How many
members of British Secret Service are on KGB payroll
as double agents?"

The machine instantly started to print out lines of
names. Row after row of them. The names had filled
up the screen twice and, in alphabetical order, they
were still in the A's.

Buell remembered he had forgotten to give the machine a limit on the number of names it could print.
He voided the instructions and asked: "How many
members of British Secret Service are *not* on KGB
payroll?"

Three names popped up on the screen instantly.
One was the deputy director of the Secret Service,
another was the agency's seventh-ranking man in Hong
Kong. The third was Pamela Thrushwell, computer
analyst.

Buell sat back in surprise and stared at the name.
So Thrushwell was a British agent. That explained
why she had been hanging on to this Remo so persist-
ently to try to track down Buell.

She must have been trying to track him down since
he had had that lark, messing around with Britain's
government computers and almost moving the government into a friendship treaty with Russia. Thrushwell
must have been assigned to find out how to plug that
hole in the computer system.

A spy. And he had thought of her as just a nice-
looking blond with an interesting accent and wonder-

ful breasts. That's what he got for underestimating
women.

Marcia came into the room with food on a tray for
him. She was wearing a long diaphanous white gown
of some thin gauze. She was naked beneath it and
Buell felt an unaccustomed faint stirring of desire. He
reached out and cupped a hand around her right
buttocks. She smiled at him, tossed her red hair, and
nodded toward the television monitor.

"What's that list?" she asked.

"It wouldn't interest you," he said.

"Everything about you interests me," she said.
"Really, what is it?"

"It's a list of the three British secret agents who
don't work for the Russians."

Marcia smiled, her full lips pulling back to expose
long pearly teeth. "Only three?" she said.

He nodded. "Those are the three who don't work
for the Russians. I don't know. They might be double
agents for somebody else. For Argentina, for all I
know." He kneaded her buttocks with his fingers. "I
think I want you," he said.

"I always want you," she said. "I am here to serve
you."

"I want you to go to the bedroom and put on a
T-shirt and wait for me."

"Just a T-shirt?"

"Yes. A wet one. I want it wet and transparent."
She nodded submissively and looked at the screen
again.

"That name. Pamela. Isn't she the woman who's
following you?"

"Yes," he said.

"Isn't that dangerous? To have her looking for you
along with the Americans?"

"It doesn't matter. I'm going to get rid of all of them," he said.

"Us too," Marcia said with a smile. "You promised. Us too."

"I'll keep my promise," Buell said. "When the world goes, we go with it."

"You're so wonderful," she said.

"There's nothing left in life," he said. "I've played all the games. There's no one who can even challenge me."

Marcia nodded. "I'll go put on that wet T-shirt," she said.

"Quick. Before the mood passes," Buell said.

It was well after dark when the telephone in Smith's office rang.

"This is Buell. Have you decided?"

"Yes," Smith said. "I accede to your demand."

"That easily? No negotiations? No hard bargaining?"

"Do I have anything to bargain with?"

"No. And I'm glad you realize it. That's one of the nicer qualities of you bureaucratic types," Buell said. "You never try to fight the inevitable."

Smith said nothing and the silence hung in his office like a small cloud of smoke.

Buell finally said, "There are certain things I want."

"Which are?"

"I want to see it done so I know it's not some kind of trick. After all, this Remo's been pestering *me*. I deserve to see him go."

"Tell me what you want," Smith said.

"There's a small town in California named Hernandez," Buell began and gave Smith directions to a clearing where he wanted Remo killed. "Tomorrow at high noon," he said.

"All right," Smith said. He suppressed a small smile, even though he felt he deserved one. Buell had made a mistake.

"How are you going to do it?" Buell asked.

"By hand," Smith said.

"I don't think you can do it," Buell said. "I've seen this guy Remo. He's hard to beat."

"I can beat him," Smith said.

"I'll believe it when I see it."

"You'll see it tomorrow at noon," Smith said.

"How will I know you? What do you look like?" Buell asked.

"I'm old. I'll be wearing an ornamental Oriental robe."

"You Oriental? With a name like Smith?"

"Yes," Smith said. "Until tomorrow." And then he hung up.

And now Smith smiled.

Remo would die. There was no helping that. But so would Abner Buell. And the world would be saved.

He told himself he would make the same deal every time.

Chapter Fourteen

On the first ring of the telephone, Remo shoved Pamela Thrushwell into the bathroom. On the second ring, he broke the lock so she could not open the door. He answered the phone on the third ring.

"Did you find out where he is?" he said.

"I've found out where he will be," Smith said laconically.

"Okay. When and where?" Remo stuck a finger in his free ear to block out the thumping from the bathroom door.

"There's a small town named Hernandez . . . Remo, are you alone?"

"Not really," Remo said.

"Let me out," Pamela shrieked. "I'll call the police. I'll—" Remo threw a lamp at the door. She quieted for a moment.

"The girl?" Smith asked.

"Yes."

"Get rid of her. I told you before."

"All right, all right, I will," Remo said.

"You can't have her go with you. That's final."

"I said I'd take care of it, all right? Now where and when?"

Smith gave him the directions that he had received from Abner Buell. "Noon tomorrow," he said. "Chiun will meet you there," he added casually.

"Hold on," Remo said. "Chiun will meet me there? I thought you said I shouldn't have anybody with me."

"Chiun hardly qualifies as a pesky bystander," Smith said.

"He can be," Remo said. "And he's ticked at me anyway."

Smith sighed. Remo could visualize him at this moment, pressing the steel rings of his eyeglasses to his face with an index finger. "I thought ... this is important enough ... I thought it would be best if the two of you were there."

Pamela had started screaming again and there were no more lamps to throw.

"All right," Remo said. "I'll look for Chiun there. If he's there, we'll work it together. If not, I'll work it alone."

"At noon sharp," Smith said. "Chiun will be there."

Remo thought his voice sounded cracked and hoarse but the telephone clicked dead in his ear before he could make sure.

Smith sat at his desk for a few minutes afterward, the dead telephone cradled in his hand. Then, feeling very old and very tired, he walked to a locked cabinet and removed a Dutch Barsgod fragmenting shell pistol. The next fifteen hours were going to be the saddest of his life, but no one had ever said that saving the world would be a barrel of laughs.

The guard at Folcroft's front gate said, "Finally

going home, Dr. Smith?" and Smith almost said, "No. To save the world," but he didn't.

As had always been the case in his life, the bodies would tell where he had been and what he had been doing.

"It's about time," Pamela said after Remo freed the bathroom door and let her out. "Who was that? The President?"

"Wrong number," Remo muttered. "When I finish working the obscene-calls patrol, I'm going to get transferred to wrong numbers."

"A wrong number that you talked to for ten minutes?"

"All right. It was my Aunt Millie. She likes to talk."

"Really?" Pamela said archly. "What did you talk about?"

"She said the weather is good in Butler, Pennsylvania."

"It took her ten minutes to tell you that?"

"Yes," Remo said. "In Butler, that's big news. It's worth talking about."

"I don't believe it was your Aunt Tillie," she said. She wound a strand of Remo's jet-black hair around her finger.

"Millie," he corrected.

"Or Aunt Millie." She nuzzled his neck. "I'll bet I can make you tell me who you were really talking to," she purred.

"Not a chance," Remo said. "I'm beyond tempting."

"We'll see about that," she said. She eased him back on the bed and fiddled with the zipper of his pants.

Remo let her undress him and as her hands strayed over his body, he said, "Seduce away. It'll do you no good."

Long ago, in the early stages of his training, Chiun had taught Remo the thirty-seven steps for pleasuring a woman. They began with the inside of the left wrist and ended with the woman shrieking in ecstasy, although very few women were not shrieking in ecstasy by step seven or eight; it was a male fantasy come true, but it had also made sex boring, mechanical, and routine for Remo, and he rarely thought about it anymore.

"You like being controlled by a woman?" Pamela said as she straddled his body.

"Beats a sharp stick in the eye," he said.

She toyed with his body, with finger and tongue, then stopped. "Are you ready to tell me yet?"

"Not if you're going to stop," Remo said.

"I'll stop if you don't tell me," she threatened.

"Don't stop," Remo said.

"I will. I swear I will."

"Will you?" Remo said. He turned and touched the inside of her left wrist. He forgot the steps in order but he followed with her elbow, a spot on her right thigh, and then a cluster of nerves in the small of her back.

She moaned louder with each successive step. Her breasts were arched forward, her body twitched and convulsed with need. Remo satisfied that need, holding her down by the hands as the rest of her body bucked in a feverish, wanton frenzy.

Done, she lay exhausted on the bed, spent, glowing with perspiration. Remo touched a small nerve in her throat, toyed with it, and she closed her eyes and fell asleep.

He touched her face gently. "Maybe I'll see you again," he said softly before he left. But somehow, and he didn't know why or how, he didn't really think he would.

He was on the road to Hernandez when he understood, and so shocking was the revelation that he had to pull off to the side of the road to consider it.

Smith had been lying about Chiun's presence. Remo was sure of it, but he hadn't been able to figure out why. Now he had.

Remo was going to die.

It was part of Chiun's contract with Smith, he knew. Gold in perpetuity went to the village of Sinanju, but there was one large string attached: Chiun would have to kill Remo when Smith gave the order.

But why? He had done nothing to endanger the organization or the country. Why? He had no answer, but he knew, deep inside his mind, that Smith had given the order. And somewhere, even deeper than that, he knew that Chiun would obey it.

He felt his breath coming hot through his nostrils and looked down at his hands. His knuckles were white where they clenched the steering wheel. He was afraid.

How long had it been since he had felt fear? He couldn't remember. But it was not the fear which clawed at his stomach and tore at his throat and brought moisture to his eyes. It was sadness and the sadness was pure and terrifying.

Remo had never had a family. He had been raised by nuns in an orphanage. As a child, he'd tried to think about his parents, to imagine their faces, but there was nothing inside him. No memories, no images. Whoever had spawned and borne him had made no impression on his mind whatever.

And so he did not have a father until he was a fully

grown man and Chiun had first come into his life. Chiun had taught him how to trust, how to obey, how to believe, how to love. And now, Remo knew in the depths of his heart that the trust and obedience and belief and love had been no more real or lasting than a shower on a sunny day.

He squeezed the wheel harder. All right, he said to himself. Let him try. Remo had been a good student. He was a Master of Sinanju too and he could do most things as well as Chiun. He would fight the old man. Chiun was a great Master, but more than eight decades of his life had come and gone. Remo could win. If he attacked first, he could. . . .

He covered his face with his hands. He could never attack Chiun. Not on anyone's orders. Not for any reason.

But he could run. The thought flashed through his mind like a rocket. He could tromp on the gas pedal of this car and speed off, keep going until he reached the Atlantic Ocean, and then hop a steamer and hide out in the mountains of some obscure country. He could run and hide and run some more, run until there was no place left to go.

The rocket of an idea dulled and fizzled. Remo was not trained to be a fugitive. He had spent ten years with the Master of Sinanju so that he would also be a Master, and a Master did not run.

There was no alternative. Chiun would have to kill him, as he was bound to do.

And in the end, Remo thought, it didn't matter anyway. The most important part of him had already died.

He turned the engine back on and pressed the pedal to the floor and headed toward Hernandez.

Chapter Fifteen

In the pitch dark of a cloudless night, just before the first hint of dawn lightened the sky, Harold Smith raised his infrared binoculars to his face. The area outside Hernandez was flat and barren except for scrub grass and a few mangy bushes.

Buell would be there to see the fight; Smith knew that. And the only place to be sure to see it was from the top of the extrusion of rock that jutted up from the floor of the field. Up there, Buell would have safety and a vantage point. Smith put the night glasses away and walked toward the rock. It would be his job to make sure that Buell had no such safety.

He walked slowly around the large rock. When he was finished the first finger of dawn was tickling the sky. He could climb it. With a lot of effort, he could climb it and get to Buell.

But he wouldn't be able to climb it fast enough to save Remo.

Smith went back to his room and checked the Barsgod again. The shells were the size of shotgun shells, designed for guerrilla warfare. One strike anywhere near Buell would send enough shrapnel flying to take him out. It was all the edge Smith would need.

He tucked the gun and shells beneath his pillow and tried to sleep. He could use the few hours of rest, he knew. He was not a young man and whatever edge the Barsgod gave him could be evened out by the disadvantage of his slowed reflexes.

But after an hour of tossing and turning, he knew it would be useless. He would not sleep. Maybe he would never sleep soundly again. What he was about to do to Remo Williams would forever deny him the sleep of the innocent.

How did it happen? He asked himself again and again. Smith was not an assassin. He was an honorable man. Yet everything he had ever done to Remo had been a criminal act. He had chosen Remo for CURE because Remo had no one and nothing. And he had taken Remo's identity and his dreams and his life and had forced him into service, sending him into dangerous situations without a thought, all because Remo had been trained for the work. He had seen to it that almost every friend Remo had ever made was eliminated to protect the secrecy of CURE. And now he had ordered the final ignominy for Remo Williams. He had commanded the closest friend Remo had ever had to kill him.

How did it happen? How? When had Remo ceased to be a man to Smith and become only a tool of the organization? When had Smith forgotten that Remo, others, were human beings, not just cattle to be prodded around?

But he knew the answer to that. Human beings had ceased to matter on the day that Smith accepted his responsibility to the United States of America. In the long view, Remo's life was a small price to pay for the safety of the world.

The predawn grayness blossomed into a California sun and Smith was still awake. He wondered briefly about Chiun, but Chiun was the same kind of man Smith himself was. Chiun knew his duty and he would perform it and then he would return to Sinanju to live out the rest of his life as the venerated old man of the village.

He would also, no doubt, lie awake to the end of his days, thinking of Remo.

Smith sighed and sat up, passing his bony hands over his face. Duty was a stupid word, a stupid concept. Smith had always hated ideologues and had never thought he would be called upon to sacrifice a friend for an idea, even so lofty an idea as world peace.

How long would such a peace last anyway? he asked himself angrily. Just until the next maniac with the means to start global war came along? Until the next group of fanatics decided to sacrifice the human race for some obscure cause? What good was duty when it made a killer of you?

He walked to the window, all his anguish as meaningless as dust in the wind. He didn't have to call it duty. You could call it sanity or patriotism or mercy or sacrifice or even murder. It didn't matter. The only thing that mattered was that it had to be done and he was the one who had to do it.

Smith felt comfortable with despair. He had lived his whole life doing the right thing and he would go on doing the right thing until the day he died. And that, he knew, was the reason his life was so bare and empty.

Understanding that, he was finally able to sleep. His last thought was to wonder where Chiun was.

                              *   *   *

Unseen by Smith, Chiun had spent the night at the site of the coming battle. Wearing mourning white, the old man knelt on the bare ground in the dark and lit a candle.

It was chilly, but he did not feel the cold. He lifted his eyes to the starless cobalt sky. He prayed for a sign. To all the gods of the east and west, he begged for a release from his obligation to kill his son. For Remo was no less than a son to the old man, no less than the heir to all the knowledge and love and power Chiun had accumulated over his long lifetime.

"Help me, O gods," he said in a hoarse whisper.

And he waited.

He thought of Remo and of the legend that had brought them together, the tale written in the ancient archives of Sinanju that a Master of Sinanju would one day bring to life a dead night tiger who walked in the form of a white man but who was, in his true incarnation, Shiva the Destroyer. Remo, the man, was only the outer flesh of the sacred soul within. Chiun could kill the man, but what mortal—even the Master of Sinanju—could dare to kill Shiva?

"Help me, O gods," he said again.

The candle went out.

Patiently he lit another. A Master's word in contract was as binding as an inscription in stone. He had given his word to Smith, in exchange for enough wealth to feed the entire village of Sinanju forever.

But Smith did not know what he asked. He did not know the legend of Shiva. Men like Harold Smith did not believe such things. They only believed that the word of the Master of Sinanju was good.

"Help me, O gods," Chiun said for the third time.

A strong breeze blew out the candle again. There was no other sign.

Chiun let the candle remain extinguished. He sat alone in the dark, alone, silent.

He wept.

Chapter Sixteen

Marcia was looking at the outside world through a periscope from inside the hollow hill.

"It looks like a beautiful day," she said and giggled. "A great day for the world to end."

Buell nodded and slicked back his slicked-back hair.

"But I don't want you to just do it," she said.

"What do you mean?"

"I don't want you just to do everything and then tell me it's all done. I want to see it. Step by step," she said. "I want to see and know everything you do."

"All right," he said. "Starting now. Come on."

He rose from the small table where he had been drinking herbal tea and walked to one of the computer consoles that lined the walls of the living quarters.

He flipped on a power switch and then pressed a sequence of numbers that separated the screen into two lengthwise parts.

"Now, on the left," he said. "That's number one." He pressed more numbers and a large "ready" appeared on that half-screen. "Those are the Russian missiles," he said. "I'm already into their network. And number two . . ."

He busied himself pressing more keys on the console and finally the word "ready" appeared on the right-hand side of the screen also.

"Number two is the United States. Now both sets of missiles are ready to fire."

"How will you fire them?" she said.

"To fire Russia's, I just type onto the keyboard 'One-Fire' and the code number. That's all it takes. For America's, I type 'Two-Fire' and the code. They're already programmed and ready to go."

"How do you know where they'll go?" Marcia asked.

"I didn't have to do anything with that. Russia's are programmed to hit the U.S. America's are set to hit Russia. I just left that alone."

"Too difficult to figure out, I guess?" she said.

"Don't you believe it," he snapped. "Of course I've got it figured out. If I wanted to change anywhere these missiles should be launched, if I wanted them to go hit South Africa for instance, I would just write on the screen 'One,' then insert the latitude and longitude for South Africa, and then write 'fire.' And the missiles would go there instead."

"The same for the American missiles?" she asked.

He nodded. "Just insert the target's longitude and latitude and that'll do it. They self-correct for direction once they've been launched. I already worked out the coordinates."

"You're brilliant, Abner. Just brilliant."

"You're right," Buell said.

"You said you need the code number for firing. What's that?"

"It's in my head somewhere," he said. "I'll remember it when I need it."

"And the coordinates?" Marcia asked.

Buell flapped his arm toward the top of the computer console where piles of papers were stacked precariously. "I've got them written down somewhere. Up there. I told you, we didn't need them."

"No. Of course not," Marcia said. She stood back from Buell and as she did, she knocked over a stack of papers with her elbow.

"Clumsy," Buell muttered.

"I'm sorry." She stooped to gather the papers. When she found one with the names of cities with two simple rows of figures on it, she slipped it inside the sleeve of her blouse, then replaced the stack where it had been.

Buell had not noticed; he was calling up other numbers on the computer screen. Finally, he restored the split screen with the two Ready signals on either side. "Everything's all set for the big bang," he said.

"Good," Marcia said.

"But first we've got our entertainment outside. Let's go up," Buell said.

"I'll be up in a minute," she said. "I just want to put on a little makeup first."

"Suit yourself. Wear something nice when you come up," he said. "Maybe your cavegirl costume."

"I will," Marcia said.

When she heard the upstairs door that led outside click shut, Marcia pulled the list of coordinates from her sleeve and sat at the computer. Working swiftly and efficiently, she reprogrammed all the missiles of the United States to strike, not at Moscow and Russia, but at New York, Washington, Los Angeles, and Chicago. She did not change the trajectories of the Russian missiles. They were still aimed at the United States.

*   *   *

Harold Smith was ready. Flattened behind a small rock, he waited, his binoculars focused on the plateau above the site where the battle was to take place.

Almost at noon, a solitary figure appeared on the plateau, walked to the edge and seemed, like a military conqueror, to survey all the ground around him. Smith pressed himself close to the ground, then peered up and saw the man was sitting now in a folding lawn chair on the edge of the rock shelf. It was Abner Buell. Smith crawled silently through the grass toward the back of the hill.

When he reached the bottom of the hill, he felt for the Barsgod in his pocket. Its weight gave him a perverse satisfaction. On this day Remo would die, and Chiun would prepare to return to Korea, and Harold Smith would go back to Folcroft Sanitarium, probably never to emerge from it alive, and CURE would probably be finished. But because of the Barsgod, Buell would also die.

And the rest of the world would live.

So be it, Smith thought.

The sun was high and bright when Remo strode out into the open field to meet the diminutive figure dressed in white robes and standing as still as a statue. When he approached, Chiun bowed to him.

Remo did not return the bow. Instead, he stood like a man who had walked a thousand miles with a pack of stones upon his back. His shoulders were stooped and a deep furrow ran between his red-rimmed eyes.

"I didn't think it would ever come to this," Remo said quietly.

Chiun's face was impassive. "And what is 'this'?"

"Don't play word games with me, Little Fa ..." Remo stopped himself. His mouth twisted with bitterness. "Little Father," he finished and spat on the ground.

Chiun's eyelids fluttered but he said nothing.

"You've come to kill me," Remo said. There was no accusation in his voice, only the sorrowful sound of resignation.

"I have been so commanded," Chiun said.

"Ah, the contract," Remo said. "That's right. Money for Sinanju. Don't forget the money, Chiun. I hope you got paid in advance. Your ancestors will never forgive you if you get stiffed on this job. The great Sinanju god. Money."

"You are cruel," the old Oriental said softly.

Remo laughed, a harsh sound in the thin noon air. "Right, Chiun. You go on telling yourself that. While you're killing me, just keep thinking how cruel I am."

"I might not be able to kill you," Chiun said.

"Oh, yes, you will. But I'm not going to make it easy for you," Remo said. "I'm not fighting back."

"Like a sheep, you will stand there?" asked Chiun.

"Sheep if you want. But that's the way I want it. You're going to have to kill me where I stand."

"You are permitted to fight," Chiun said.

"And I'm also permitted not to fight. Sorry, Chiun. I'm the one who's dying. I'll pick the way."

"It is not the way of an assassin," Chiun said.

"You're the assassin, remember? Chiun, the great assassin." Remo's eyes welled with tears. "Well, I'm going to give you something to remember me by. A parting gift from your son. When you kill me, Chiun, you won't be any assassin. You'll be a butcher. That's my gift. Take it to the grave with you."

He ripped open the collar of his shirt and lifted his chin, baring his throat. "Go ahead," he said, his moist eyes fixed on the old man. "Do it now and get it over with."

"You could have lain in wait for me here," Chiun said. "You could have killed me when I arrived."

"Well, I didn't," Remo said.

"Why will you not fight me?"

"Because," Remo said.

"A typical stupid answer from a pale piece of pig's ear," Chiun snapped. "What does that mean, that 'because'?"

"Just because," Remo said stubbornly.

"Because you could not stand the thought of perhaps hurting me," the old man said.

"Not that at all," Remo said.

"It is true. You knew my mission. You could have attacked first."

Remo only looked away.

"My son," Chiun said brokenly. "Can you see there is no other way?"

"I love you, Little Father," Remo said.

"Yes," said Chiun. "And that is why you will fight me. We must not disappoint our audience."

He pulled himself up to his full height, then bowed once more to his opponent.

This time, Remo bowed back.

They were talking and Abner Buell was growing annoyed. Stop talking and fight, he mentally commanded them. He tossed his lawn chair away and sat on the edge of the cliff, his legs dangling over the side.

The old Oriental, he thought, certainly looked nothing like a Dr. Smith. But Remo, that was the Remo he had seen on his television monitors, haunting him day after day. Until today. When Remo died.

Buell saw the old Oriental bow and the bow was returned by Remo. Buell wondered if Remo knew what was going to happen to him. Probably not. Remo was just too cocky and Buell was going to enjoy seeing him go down.

The Oriental struck first. He was small, but as fast as a squirrel. He seemed to levitate from the ground, hesitate in midair for a moment, and then slash down with enough ferocity to lop off a horse's head.

The first blow missed as Remo spun away, moving so fast himself that he was almost a blur. Then he catapulted upward in a double spiral and came down with both legs drawn in. They shot out at the last moment, hitting the old man square in the stomach. A spray of bright blood shot from the Oriental's mouth. Dr. Smith staggered backward a few steps and while he was trying to get his footing, Remo came after him.

"Come on, Dr. Smith," Buell said softly. But for a moment, it looked at as if Remo had won. The old man staggered backward, ready to fall. But at the last moment, instead of going down, he sprang suddenly upward, his arms moving in front of him like blades. Remo's head snapped backward. He was trying to get away but the Oriental's hand snaked out again and before Remo could so much as turn his head, the old man had him by the throat and then yanked back hard. There was a sound like the beginning of a cry but it was choked off suddenly. Then Remo sank to his knees. At the same moment, the old man raised his arm high. In his hand was the bubbly, bloody interior of Remo's throat.

Buell gave a whoop of triumph and leapt to his feet. "I won," he shouted. It did not bother him at all when his champion, the old Oriental, weaved on his feet, dropped the dripping mess in his hand to the ground, and collapsed in a heap. The sunlight glinted off a trickle of slick blood pouring from his mouth.

"Kee-rist," Buell said between his teeth. "That Dr. Smith is some fighter."

"His name's not Smith," said a soft voice behind him. Buell whirled around. On the opposite side of the rock shelf was a gray-haired middle-aged man wearing wire-rimmed glasses and a three-piece suit. In his right hand was a pistol that seemed the size of an electric drill.

"What'd you say?" Buell asked.

"I said his name's not Smith. Mine is."

A confused smile came to Buell's face but when the barrel of the oversized gun did not waver, the smile faded. The man with the gun was not joking and behind his steel-rimmed spectacles, his eyes held the kind of desperation that made killers of ordinary men.

"What's this about?" Buell asked, swallowing hard.

Smith's eyes wandered for a fraction of a second to the two bodies lying motionless on the field below. "It's about sanity," he rasped.

"Come on," Buell began but Smith cut him short.

"I know sanity isn't a big part of your life," Smith said. "Not somebody who's willing to blow up the world because it's some kind of game. Some of us don't think the world's safety is a game. So some of us are willing to kill for it." He glanced down again. "Even to die for it."

"If you're Smith, who are those two?"

"They worked for me," Smith said. "Enough explanations."

He started to tighten his finger on the trigger but before he could, a strong arm was clamped around his throat. A gun was pressed against his temple.

"Not just yet," said a woman's voice. "Drop it."

Smith heard the gun against his head cock. There was more than just one of them. He could still get Buell, but this one would get him and the end of the world might just proceed on schedule. He had to wait. Try to get them both.

He lowered the Barsgod and tossed it away, toward Buell.

"You have all sorts of talents, Marcia," Buell said, as the woman released her hold on Smith's neck. "Hey, I said the cavegirl costume."

Smith turned and saw a woman in slacks and a white blouse. She said to Buell, "We can stow all that sex-kitten crap now, Buell."

Smith backed away from the woman. Buell looked surprised, then shrugged and walked over to pick up the Barsgod. The Russian-made Tokarev .38 in the woman's hand fired and took a crease out of the surface of the rock near Smith's weapon.

"Leave it alone, Abner," she said. She aimed the Tokarev squarely at Buell's chest. "I want the code that activates the missiles," she said. Smith thought her eyes were as dark and deadly as a shark's.

"What is this?" Buell said in bewilderment. "Are you with him?"

The woman named Marcia smiled. "I am with the Committee for State Security of the Union of Soviet Socialist Republics," she said proudly.

"You're a Russian? KGB?" Buell said.

"Why else would I have spent so much time with the likes of you?" she spat. "May I remind you, Abner, that time is of the essence? And I do have this gun. The code numbers, please."

"But the missiles are set to blow up Moscow too," Buell said.

"Not anymore. The American missiles have been

redirected. Each of their missiles will strike an American city."

"Then think about yourself," Buell said desperately. "If they all go off in this country, you'll go too. You'll be incinerated."

"And Russia will rule the world," she said. "It is a small price to pay, to die for so glorious a cause."

"Then pay it now," came another voice. Smith wheeled as another figure hopped up onto the small plateau. It was a blond-haired woman with a British accent, and she moved quickly into a marksman's position and fired without hesitation at the Russian woman.

Even before Pamela Thrushwell's gun sounded, Marcia had fired. Both women careened backward as if two giant hands had slapped them off their feet. Pamela's abdomen was torn open in a red burst of blood and entrails; the Russian woman's once-spectacular face was an unrecognizable blob. Her legs twitched weakly, reflexively, once; then she lay still.

Smith started toward Buell, but the thin young man was holding the Barsgod.

"These women need help," Smith said.

"They'll get help in heaven," Buell said. "We all will, and we'll all be there soon."

"You're crazy," Smith said.

"Just bored," Buell said. A smile crossed his unlined face. "You know, I don't think I'll kill you after all. I think I'll just have you wait here with me for the big fireball in the sky. Would you like that?"

"You don't have a chance," Smith said.

"Why not?"

Smith started walking slowly toward Marcia. Her gun lay alongside her dead body.

"Because you can't stop me from doing what I want to do," Smith said. "That gun isn't loaded."

"We'll see about that," Buell said. He pointed the gun at the ground. Smith stopped and watched. Buell squeezed the trigger. The gun fired, the bullet hit the rocky plateau, and Smith dove behind Marcia's body. The plateau exploded with a rush of sound and the shell shattered, sending jagged pieces of metal scattering everywhere, twinkling in the reflecting sunshine like a shower of stars. The body shielding Smith thunked as shell fragments tore into it.

One of the pieces kicked back and embedded in Abner Buell's brain. He dropped the Barsgod and sank slowly to his knees. His body twitched, and then there was another muffled explosion, as the fragment itself exploded again, this time inside Buell's brain. He pitched forward, his face hitting the rock. He did not move.

Smith raised himself slowly from the ground, stunned that he himself was unharmed, that all the shrapnel had missed him. Buell's head looked like a macabre Halloween mask. The eyes had been exploded from their sockets. His teeth lay like charred kernels of corn on the ground beside him. His slicked hair was now matted red and flecked with bits of soft gray tissue, spilled over from his brain through the gaping hole in the top of his skull.

Shaking violently, Smith stood up to full height. Don't lose it now, he told himself. He had been prepared for death, but death had passed him by. Now he had to force his thoughts to other things. Like dismantling Buell's computer. Like ending the sequence that would result in Russia and America both firing their missiles into America's heartland. That had to be done first.

He owed it. To a lot of people. To Remo and to Chiun.

He shielded his eyes from the sun and looked over the cliff's edge down toward the field. The two bodies appeared to have vanished.

Who could have taken them?

He scanned the horizon, feeling a rising tide of anxiety well up inside him. For some reason, losing their *bodies* seemed as tragic as losing the men themselves. Remo and Chiun had been sacrificed for the most worthy of causes; even in Smith's last day in hell, he would be able to say that much in defense of himself. But to lose their *bodies* . . .

He was filled with shame and he could do nothing else but sink to the ground, surrounded by the three grotesquely mutilated corpses, and cry like a lost child.

He sobbed for Remo, the innocent he had betrayed so easily; for Chiun, whom he had forced, in his old age, to kill his own son; and he wept for himself, a tired, bitter old man, who no longer dreamed dreams but only lived nightmares.

He never heard the footsteps approaching. But then, no one ever heard them.

"Ever wish you had a camera?" It was Remo's voice.

Smith looked up as Chiun clucked disdainfully. They both stood in front of Smith.

"You're alive," he said.

"Most perceptive, Emperor," said Chiun fawningly, bowing low.

"I mean . . ." He stopped and stood up and swiped quickly at his eyes with his sleeve. "I had something in my eye. I couldn't get it out." Without waiting for an answer, he pointed to the blood on Chiun's hands. "I saw it," he said. "The fight."

Chiun gasped when he saw the blood and quickly

tucked his hands into the sleeves of his kimono. "Forgive me, Most Observant One," he said. "In my haste, I forgot to remove the chicken-liver juice." He turned his back to Smith, spat on his hands and rubbed them energetically together.

Smith looked to Remo, but Remo had gone.

Stifling a small cry, Remo had run across the face of the rock to where Pamela lay and knelt alongside her body. Smith saw him feel for a pulse and then Chiun came beside him and tore off part of his robe. He made a pad to soak up the young British woman's blood, but within seconds the pad itself was sopped wet. Chiun shook his head to Remo.

"Why'd you come, you pain in the ass?" Remo said chokingly to Pamela.

Her face strained. With an effort, she forced her eyes open.

"Don't talk," Remo said.

"Must," she said. Blood bubbled from a corner of her mouth. "Did we get him?" she asked.

"We got him," Remo said. "You didn't have to come for me," he said.

"Not for you. For England. It was my job. Did we save the world?"

"Yeah, Pamela," Remo said. "We done good. How'd you find me?"

"Bribed clerk at motel. Listened in on your phone call. Told me where." She tried to smile and her mouth leaked blood. "Always knew you were a liar."

Remo clenched his jaw. The skin over her eyelids was starting to discolor. She would be gone soon.

"Saved your friend's life," she said.

Remo thought: I wish I could save yours. But he only nodded.

"We got it done," Pamela said. Her voice was growing inaudible. Remo leaned closer and she said, "Remo."

"What?"

"Do it again, will you?"

"Do what?"

Slowly, with hands as weak as a baby's, she guided his hand toward her left wrist. It barely grazed her skin when the life went out of her eyes.

Remo stood, his own eyes moist. As he looked down at the body, Smith heard him mumble, "That's the biz, sweetheart."

Remo and Chiun went into Buell's underground fortress with Smith to make sure there were no other people hiding in there.

The subterranean apartment was empty and Smith marveled at the computers.

"Good God," he said. "These have every detail of the Russian and American defense systems inside them."

He jiggled and prodded the console keyboard, and occasionally emitted a soft exclamation of wonder.

Finally he picked up a telephone.

"Calling for help?" Remo said.

Smith gazed at him blandly. "Calling Folcroft. I've set these up so that my computers can strip them and absorb everything they've got."

"You don't need us anymore?" Remo said.

"No. I can handle this alone. You can go."

"All right," Remo said. At the doorway that led up to the rock plateau, he turned and said, "Smitty. Why were you crying before?"

Smith said, "I told you. I had something in my eye," and he turned back to the console.

*   *   *

"Would you have killed me?" Remo asked Chiun as they walked across the grassy field below the small mountain.

"Would the robin pluck the worm from the ground?"

"What does that mean?" Remo said.

"It means would the tide betray the moon who leads it to land?"

"Huh?"

"You are uneducable," Chiun said.

They passed a rise overlooking the nearby highway.

"So would you have killed me?"

"Keep flapping your big mouth and find out," Chiun said.

They got into Remo's car.

"I don't think you would have," Remo said as he started the engine.

Chiun grunted.

"Because you love me," Remo said.

Chiun grunted.

"You do love me."

The old man rolled his eyes heavenward.

"Don't you?" Remo demanded.

"Yak, yak, yak," Chiun shrieked, bouncing up and down on his seat. "You are the noisiest white thing who ever lived. Love you? It takes all one's will merely to tolerate you."

Remo smiled and drove onto the highway.

About the Authors

WARREN MURPHY has written eighty books in the last twelve years. His novel, *Trace,* was nominated for the best book of the year by The Mystery Writers of America. He is a native and resident of New Jersey.

RICHARD SAPIR is a writer for The Destroyer series and author of *The Far Arena*. He is a graduate of Columbia University and formerly a journalist and editor. Mr. Sapir is a native of New York and lives in New Hampshire.

The Destroyer Questionnaire

Help us bring you more of the books you like by filling out this survey and mailing it in today.

1. Book Title: _____

   Book #: _____

2. Using the scale below, how would you rate this book on the following features? Please write in one rating from 0-10 for each feature in the spaces provided.

POOR	NOT SO GOOD		AVERAGE			GOOD		EXCEL-LENT	
0	1	2	3	4	5	6	7	8	9	10

RATING

Overall opinion of book .... _____
Plot/Story .... _____
Setting/Location .... _____
Writing Style .... _____
Dialogue .... _____
Suspense .... _____
Conclusion/Ending .... _____
Character Development .... _____
Hero .... _____
Scene on Front Cover .... _____
Colors of Front Cover .... _____
Back cover story outline .... _____
First page excerpts .... _____

3. How likely are you to buy another title in *The Destroyer* series? (Circle one number on the scale below.)

DEFI-NITELY NOT BUY	PROB-ABLY NOT BUY		NOT SURE			PROB-ABLY BUY		DEFI-NITELY BUY	
0	1	2	3	4	5	6	7	8	9	10

4. Listed below are various Action Adventure lines. Rate only those you have read using the 0-10 scale below.

	POOR		NOT SO GOOD		AVERAGE			GOOD		EXCEL-LENT
	0	1	2	3	4	5	6	7	8	9	10

RATING

Able Team .... _____

Death Merchant .... _____

Destroyer .... _____

Dirty Harry .... _____

Mack Bolan (Executioner) .... _____

Penetrator .... _____

Phoenix Force .... _____

Specialist .... _____

Survivalist .... _____

_____ _____

_____ _____

5. Where do you usually buy your books (check one or more):

( ) Bookstore   ( ) Discount Store
( ) Supermarket   ( ) Department Store
( ) Variety Store   ( ) Other: _____
( ) Drug Store

6. What are the names of two of your favorite magazines?

1) _____
2) _____

7. What is your age? _____   Sex: ( ) Male
                                                                  ( ) Female

8. Marital Status: Education:

( ) Single   ( ) Grammar school or less
( ) Married   ( ) Some high school
( ) Divorced   ( ) H.S. graduate
( ) Separated   ( ) 2 yrs. college
( ) Widowed   ( ) 4 yrs. college

If you would like to participate in future research projects, please complete the following:

PRINT NAME: _____

ADDRESS: _____

CITY: _____ STATE _____ ZIP _____

PHONE: ( ) _____

Thank you. Please send to: New American Library, Action Adventure Research Dept., 1633 Broadway, New York, New York 10019.